RISE

RAVIN TIJA MAURICE

Rise

Copyright 2021 by Ravin Tija Maurice

First Edition

Edited by Lawrence Maurice

Cover and Formatting

10 9 8 7 6 5 4 3 2 1

ALSO BY RAVIN TIJA MAURICE

CAMILLE BISHOP

PROPHECY GIRL
BELIEVER
RISE

THE AFFLICTED SERIES

REBIRTH
IKON
INHERITANCE

To Michael, with love.

1.

It only takes a second. One tiny moment for your entire life to change.

My entire life changed. Multiple times. The universe continually flipped it on its head, then flat on its back like a goddamn turtle so I struggled to get back up. But this time….

I got to my limit. Every time I thought I could not take on one more thing the universe would flip me off and say 'Hey! Let's test that theory'.

The urge to smash my phone hummed through me. But

that would not erase the truth. The final fucking betrayal. The most horrible thing that Jesse did behind my back in a long list of shitty things you just don't do to someone you 'love'.

I should email her back with the full compilation. See if she's down to trade.

I DID NOT KNOW HE WAS DEAD UNTIL I BUMPED INTO ROLLO LAST WEEK. HIS SON SHOULD HAVE BEEN AT HIS FUNERAL. HIS SON SHOULD MEET HIS GRANDPARENTS AND UNCLE. MUNCHIE WAS SUCH A NICE KID. I HOPE JESSE'S DEATH DIDN'T BREAK HIM.

Her familiarity with Jesse's family unsettled me. His nickname for his younger brother was something I only heard maybe once or twice. She knew *a lot*.

If I do email her back, I will pass on his parents contact info.

No. I will email her back. It's not her fault. My curiosity and deep self loathing wanted to know how he behaved when they were together. Perhaps the drug addicted narcissist was also exclusive to me.

I'M SORRY, CAMILLE. I'M SORRY TO DO THIS TO YOU NOW. I'M SORRY HE DID THIS TO BOTH OF US. ONLY SOMEONE WHO EXPERIENCED THIS CAN UNDERSTAND, SO I THOUGHT WE SHOULD SPEAK.

Gotta love when someone claims to feel bad for destroying another person, as long as they feel better. Like our pain is somehow comparable. Like our suffering is on par because we both made the dumb ass mistake of caring for that loser.

What a joke.

She wants to talk to me, we'll talk. She may regret it after but hey, she wanted to *talk*. Knowing my luck, she's looking for money.

I so wished I could wring his scrawny neck. Never ever in my life would I describe myself as a violent person, but this man brought out such anger in me it changed *me*. Focusing on his face, on wrapping my hands around his throat and squeezing, I screamed for him.

"JESSE!" My yell felt like it ruptured the sound barrier. Picturing him in my mind, I thought of pulling him to me with some added force, like the magical equivalent of grabbing him by his collar.

Dragging him from hell to answer for his sins didn't sound like a bad idea.

My eyes got milky, and anger began to fill me. By the time he shimmered into existence it felt as if my rage bonded with my blood and became part of my being.

"Hey babe," his expression looked bright and cheerful until he saw my face. "What did I do now?"

"Damien." I could barely say the name as I choked back my emotions.

"Who told you?"

Completely shocked by his response, I only managed to say she emailed. How she got the address could be easily guessed but I did not know specifics.

"*I hate you.*" The words spat like a curse from my lips, and a wave of calm washed over me. Like speaking the truth finally gave me some relief. Finally set me free. "You destroyed me. How am I ever supposed to trust another human being again? All these years and you played me for a fool. I made all these stupid plans for our future, and you were fucking with me the whole damn time. Like I wasn't even a person. How could I be so stupid?"

He stared blankly at me; the silence hung around us like it was its own person. A separate form in the room with us.

Hopefully it took my side and choked the shit out of the bastard.

"The worst part is how *she* explained to *me* that *you loved us both*. And, AND! When she told you she was pregnant you wouldn't leave me."

"Some people would be flattered I chose them."

"Flattered? Flattered that you abandoned your child so you could continue to treat me like garbage? You got a lot of fucking nerve. *You* chose *me?* Like you're such a fucking prize."

He lowered his head.

"*Look at me*!" My screams were glass shattering. His head shot right back up.

"I *hate* you. Do you hear me? I hope you rot in hell. If I could banish you there myself, I would." I stopped, thinking hard for a moment. "Scratch that. If I can't find a way, *I'll make one*. Now get out of my sight and don't ever come back."

"Camille…."

"No. *Nothing* you can say will fix what you have done. You've broken me." No tears left to cry, I pushed at him with my power, using my otherworldly strength to hit him hard and fast like a bully in the school yard, and he disappeared.

My fingers pushed Millie's number in my phone without even thinking.

"Hello?" she picked up on the third ring.

"I need a spell." I growled through clenched teeth.

"Why? What for?"

"To banish…."

"Is the demon back?" she blurted out before I could continue. Bliss's possession remained a secret.

"No. I need to banish what's left of my piece of shit ex-boyfriend to the lowest circle of hell."

She sighed. "What happened?"

"Beyond his normal list of bullshit? He got another girl pregnant while we were together. And ABANDONED the kid so he could keep fucking with me. He doesn't deserve *any* kind of peace or quiet or…. fuck him! It's not fair! He needs to suffer like I've suffered. *Like I'm suffering.*"

"I know. I agree. But all banishing him would do at this point is fuck with your karma. You want true vengeance? Never summon him again. Never even think of him again. Being alone in the in between for eternity is a pretty shitty existence and does not hurt you."

She was right but I still didn't like it. My anger burned so hot I only cared about hurting him like I hurt. *Destroying* him like he destroyed me.

I took a calming breath in and out. "Ok. I hear what you're saying. I'm upset…. I mean, how can I not be? I never thought my heart could break any more than it did with *all* the other shit he did to me. But the fact that he loved her, got her pregnant than *abandoned* them to continue to fuck with me is horrifying."

She was silent for a few moments. The knowledge of how totally fucky the situation sounded wasn't lost on me.

"I don't expect you to have all the answers. Or any of the answers." I hoped she could hear me as my voice grew quiet.

"Have you talked to Eric?" The mere mention of his name ground the broken pieces of my heart into the ground.

"No. And I'm not sure I want to. It's bloody embarrassing. I'm sure he is getting tired of the *poor little prophecy girl* crap."

"Camille, I highly doubt that. Eric is a kind man. And he cares for you. I'm so sorry I can't do more."

"I know. Sorry I called you freaking out. I'll talk to you tomorrow." I hung up before she could continue.

My brain began to swirl with possibilities. Millie was right. I didn't like it, but I knew it.

Although it didn't mean I wasn't going to make a plan to do exactly what I wanted, even if I never went through with it.

"Lilly? Lilly, are you there?" Calling out a name into the dark still felt weird. My eyes grew milky, and I blinked hard, shedding a single tear from each eye.

"What's up, buttercup?" Lilly Darling popped into existence sitting crossed legged on my desk.

"Remember how you said you'd teach me all the things that Millie and Eric are too vanilla to teach me?" I perched on the edge of my bed across from her. "Well, I need a spell. And they're too chicken shit to give it to me. Will you?"

Lilly chuckled. "Well, look whose coming over to the dark side. What you need, Skywalker?"

"I need something that can banish my dead ex-boyfriend to the lowest ring of hell that I can get him to. Ring, layer, level, you get the picture. As low as he can get."

She grinned at me like the goddamn Cheshire Cat. "Atta girl! I got just the thing."

"You're not worried about my karma or some shit?"

Lilly paused, examining my face. "Are you?"

"Should I be?"

She put the tip of her index finger to her lips like she was thinking, never taking her eyes off me.

"What did he do?"

"Got another girl pregnant while we were together and *abandoned* them so he could continue to be a drug addicted asshole and treat me like garbage."

Once the words were out of my mouth I dropped on my bedroom floor, like my body just said *Fuck You World! I'm done!* And bailed, causing me to hit the dirt like a sack of potatoes.

Lilly watched me curiously from her now designated perch on my desk. It wasn't a particularly sympathetic look either.

"What the hell are you doing?" she asked.

"I am so fucking done." The words were monotonous and deadpan.

"What the hell are you talking about? Seriously dude, you need to grow a pair. I figured *blanchmains* would be a bad ass. You're like a fucking wet noodle."

"I know. I'm pathetic, right? Probably how I get fucked with so easy."

She sighed loudly. "Get up, man. This is ridiculous. It's time to take your fucking power back. I don't think you really get how powerful you actually are. You can do shit people can't even dream of. What do you know about Nimue?"

"Not a lot. She trapped Merlin in a cave, didn't she?"

"Here lies another problem. No one seems to have bothered to educate you on your family history." She paused for a few minutes. "Could you summon Nimue?"

"You want me to summon a thirteenth century sorceress?" Getting up, I mirrored her sitting on my bed. "Would we even understand each other? I know it's all English, but it's changed quite a lot since then."

"Because of who you are, I believe you'll understand each other, but I'll look into it." She groaned loudly, running her hands through her hair. "What do you know about blood magic?"

"Not a goddamn thing."

She smiled. "Good."

2.

Lilly delivered on what she said, explaining to me exactly how to do the banishment if I ever decided to go through with it. She briefly explained blood magic – which basically involved using your own blood to up the power of a spell – and I told her I would educate myself.

Trying to keep a little pep in my step, I forced myself to smile when I came down to breakfast. My uncle was a good man, sometimes too good, and I knew if I told him that Jesse fathered this 'child' that he would want to look into it, and I so wasn't ready for that.

To my surprise, a girl that I didn't know sat next to Cuddy at the breakfast table. They both turned and smiled at me, showing lots of teeth, and when she lifted her hand to wave in greeting the white glyph tattoo on her wrist glowed. My forced smile got even bigger; a wave of hot rage made my face flush.

"Morning Cas." Cuddy could be nothing but his consistently chipper self. "This is my friend Maritza.

Maritza, this is my cousin Camille that I told you about. She's a P.I, she works with my dad."

Had this girl spent the night and I didn't know it? "Nice to meet you, Maritza. I didn't hear you come in."

"Oh, I only got here like fifteen minutes ago," she replied. "Christian wanted me to meet you all and figured breakfast was the best time. And I think it's *so* cool that you all are P. I's!"

"Did you hear that, Camille? It's *so cool.*" Uncle Ted laughed. "Sorry to burst your bubble, Maritza, but it's not like the movies or TV shows. Which reminds me, I have to go print something out. I'll be right back. Hurry up and eat, Cas."

"Shit! So do I!" Cuddy leaned a little closer to Maritza. "Don't worry, my cousin doesn't bite. I'll be right back."

Both men quickly left the room, and I closed the distance between me and the girl, making sure I sat as close to her as I could.

"Nice tat you've got on your wrist." I lifted my hand just slightly above my head and a knife came shooting out of the butcher block, straight into my grip. My fingers wrapping tightly around the handle. Slamming it hard into the tabletop, it stood on its tip just mere centimetres from Maritza's outstretched hand. "Wanna tell me what the fuck you are doing with my cousin?"

"My queen sent me. She wants me to keep an eye on you while we figure out exactly what you did to Bliss Fiori." The mention of my former friend's name made a line of white begin to spread from my fingertip and up my arm.

"Your cousin being a great guy is an added bonus."

I twisted the knife handle a bit. "If you so much as cough in his direction in a way that I don't like I swear...."

"Oh, I have no intentions of hurting *him*," she said with a grin. "But if we can't fix what you did to my *hermana bruja* I am under orders to take you to my Queen for punishment."

Leaning back, I pulled the knife from the table and sent it to its place. Laughter began to bubble up from deep inside me, she watched me in complete shock. Girlie caught me on the *wrong* morning.

"You know your girl is a snake, right? Fucked me over royally. Tell your Queen. I would not have done what I did if she hadn't betrayed me to the Kinkaid's and almost killed my friend." Her eyes grew wide as I spoke. "Oh, did you not know that part? She kidnapped one of my techs and burned down her University of Toronto lab. For *Tobias fucking Kinkaid*. Kind of makes you want to vomit, doesn't it? And just so you know," I put my hand up beside my mouth and whispered, "You don't scare me, little girl."

My laughter grew louder as Cuddy came back into the kitchen.

"Everything good?" He asked, his eager little face reminding me of our childhood. My urge to immediately eliminate her to protect him started to itch at the back of my brain; it took a lot of energy to suppress it. Making sure my hands were in the pockets of my sweater, I smiled back at him.

"All good. Is Maritza taking you to school today?" I asked.

"Yep, which reminds me, we have to go." He kissed the top of my head, keeping his hand on my shoulder as Maritza left the table. They both gathered their things, saying bye to Ted when he returned to the kitchen before heading out. Part of me wanted to run after him, to slaughter that girl before she could ever even think about hurting him.

Ted eyed me suspiciously. "She seems nice."

I snorted. "Says you."

"What? What did I miss?"

"Are you vetting her when we get to work or am I?" I got up from the table and began to gather my things.

He stopped me. "He is going to have a girlfriend at some point, Cas. I am just happy he is bringing them home. It was only the first meeting; she was probably very nervous. Finding out your new boyfriend's family can watch your every move undetected is a little intimidating. Not to mention that we can dig up secrets."

Mulling over what he said, I smiled to myself. "Good point."

Not seeing any evidence that Eric arrived yet, I went straight to my office when we arrived at L&B. With a little work I found a few websites about blood magic that didn't sound like an udder crock. A quarter of the way through the first site Ramona paged me to let me know a client was waiting to see me. Closing my laptop, I stood so I could shake the person's hand, surprised by the man who walked through my doorway.

To call him good looking would be a gross

understatement. Tall with short wavy dark hair cropped close to his head, just long enough to curl slightly, and dark brown eyes that gave him an amazing smoulder walked into my office.

Good lord. I have never seen a dude who smoulders like this guy.

"Hi I'm Camille." Hopefully my grin wasn't too ridiculous.

"Hey Camille. I'm Lorcan Fitzpatrick." He shook my hand before sitting down, a strong grip with soft hands.

"Fitzpatrick? As in Liam Fitzpatrick?" I asked.

He sighed. "Yep. That's my dad."

"Ok. Well, you know you didn't need to come to the office if you needed something right? I'm sure your dad...."

He smiled, and my heart skipped a beat. "See, that's the thing. I don't want my dad to know that we're talking, and if I hire you officially you are bound by client privilege, right?"

I smiled. I liked this one. "Absolutely. Hopefully it's nothing I could get in trouble with your dad or the pack for?"

"I'm the heir apparent," he smiled slyly at me. "My Dad may get annoyed, but he'll get over it. It's not *that* serious."

"So, it's about a girl?"

"What was your first clue?" he ran his hand through his hair, his eyes shifting away from me.

I pulled out a notepad from in my desk. Resting the pen on top, I eased back in my chair to listen. Surely this would be interesting, and possibly rather amusing.

"So, I met this girl, and we clicked. I mean, we clicked in a way that I have never clicked with anyone. We spent a bunch of time together and then she ghosted."

"Maybe you didn't click like you thought you did."

He chuckled, his eyes widening a bit. I caught a quick glimmer of fear in his gaze, the look of a man used to getting what he wanted and clearly not handling it well that he didn't.

"Oh, trust me. We did. Something must have happened." He shifted in the chair. "I just need you to find her, then I can do the talking."

"What was she?" I asked.

"What do you mean?"

"Could she have...I'm new to this, so I don't know what the word is. Bamboozled you? Bewitched you?"

He laughed again, this time his arrogance started to show. "Absolutely not. I am 90% sure she was human. And if she wasn't she was powerful enough to be able to hide what she was from me. That's not easily done."

His power crept up around me and I felt it brush up against mine; this strange magnetism that felt very primal, and strong.

"Did your dad tell you anything about me?" I asked him.

"Sure did. That's why I'm here."

"Great. So, you know how new this is to me?" His expression showed that Liam left out a few key elements to my story. "I have only known about all of this for literally like a month. So, all this," I gestured widely, "is kind of lost on me. Where did you meet her? I am guessing that you're also here because Daddy would not approve."

"Promise you won't laugh?"

"Sorry, I can't."

"Fine. I met her at a bachelor party."

"So, she's a stripper?" I started to laugh but covered my mouth.

"I prefer the term 'dancer' but yes. She's only doing it to pay her way through school."

"Now that makes me laugh. In my experience, that's the story that lots of strippers give. Sometimes it's genuine, other times not so much. I don't see why those who enjoy it don't just cop to it. I see no shame in that. What club does she work for?" I asked, this time lifting my pen.

"Ren. Do you know it?" I tried to hide my facial expression after he said the name.

Of course, it had to be Ren. It always leads back to fucking Ren.

"Yeah, I do. What's her name? Can you give me a physical description?"

"Her name is Meg. And I can do better. I'll send you a picture." He grabbed his phone out of his pocket, and after telling him my email he sent photos. "Sorry that some of them are.... provocative."

"What is it exactly that you want me to do, Mr. Fitzpatrick?"

"Please call me Lorcan. I want you to find her, and in her habits find me a chance to randomly bump into her. Is that cool, Miss. Bishop? Or does it come across as desperate?"

"If you want me to call you Lorcan then you really should call me Camille. And yeah, I can locate her." I wrote some things down and, more importantly, did not speak my mind. Thinking for a few moments, I looked up at him and said, "Would a locator spell not do the same thing?"

"I don't have access to magic."

"But surely it must be easier and cheaper to access spell casters?"

"It's like I said when I got here. You're bound by confidentiality. Them, not so much. And you never told me your opinion."

"Well, Lorcan, you're not paying me for my opinion. I know this may be a weird question, but isn't there a princess or something that you're supposed to marry? I figured the heir apparent would have a string of eligible women fawning at their feet."

He laughed again, a little colour just touching his cheeks. Lorcan didn't seem like the type who would actively pursue a girl in any way unless her presence changed him.

"Girls throw themselves at me all the time. But they don't want me, they want *me*." He gestured at himself. "They have no interest in me as a person, only what I signify."

"I am new to this world, so I don't totally get it."

"You're part of a prophecy. You'll get it. Eventually." His tone seemed almost amused, like what came next for me made him laugh. "I would just like to be with someone who wants Lorcan, not Lorcan Fitzpatrick, heir to the Southern Ontario Wolf Pack."

Not having asked Liam the size of his actual territory, I

gasped a little. Southern Ontario covered a lot of landscape, which explained why Liam wielded so much power. You needed to be King Shit to rule that much space with that many different cities.

"So, what happens in the North?" I asked.

"Because there is so much open space it's different rules. Another pack governs the North."

"Right. Ok. So, I will locate this girl for you. Should I ask the dumb question of why you haven't gone back to Ren looking for her?"

He smiled. "I did. Sent my buddies in too. She hasn't been there."

I sighed. I *really* didn't want to go to Ren. "Alright, I'll find her. But if you do anything fucky I am telling your dad. Are we clear?"

"What do you mean 'fucky'?"

"If I find her for you and you do something bad to her, I will tell your dad. Are we clear?"

"Crystal. You can trust me." He smiled and stuck out his hand for me to shake it.

"My receptionist informed you of my fee?" I smiled a big toothy grin at him.

"Of course." Extending my hand to him, he quickly snatched it up and sniffed the inside of my wrist. It took some effort for me to remain expressionless; I knew this as something shifters and vampires did but never experienced it firsthand. He did not seem bothered that my hand looked like I dipped it in a glass of milk.

"Well, it was lovely to meet you. Hopefully I will have

something soon." I stood up and went to step forward so I could slide over my desk.

"Call me when you do. I'm hopeful that I'm not wrong." He smiled and waved, leaving the door open slightly as he left.

A figure walked past my door and excitement rushed through me. My insides tingled and I knew that Eric arrived. Climbing out from behind my desk, I quietly crept down the hall towards his office.

His back was turned when I got to his doorway. His black leather jacket seemed perfectly cut and framed his broad shoulders. His short dark hair looked still damp in the back from when he showered this morning, he smelled like cinnamon and cloves.

I paused before I approached, unsure if I did what I felt in my heart if I would be rejected. With him being older than me, I often worried that the novelty would wear off, that he would figure out that I'm a total spaz and run like hell. It'd only been a few months since all the craziness went down; since Jesse died, since Bliss's cross to the dark side, and since I became the prophecy girl. Our relationship just started.

He turned around and I felt my eyes widen as he stared at me, totally confused.

"Good morning." He said, and I felt like an idiot.

My cheeks got a little hot. "Good morning. Sorry, I was going to...but I didn't know if you'd be cool with it, so I didn't, then you turned around and yeah."

Eric took two steps in my direction, stretching out his

left hand and using it to close the door behind me. Once I heard the click his hand caressed the back of my head, entwining his fingers in my hair. He pulled me closer, my heart fluttering in my chest as he leaned down and kissed me.

His lips were soft, and my hands moved up to his collar in an attempt to pull him closer. All the nonsense and shit that happened since last night just faded away, leaving only me and him.

"Wanna hang out later?" I asked when he pulled away. "Or now? Let's go now. I can say we have to do shit for my new client...."

"You mean Lorcan Fitzpatrick?" Eric asked, backing up a little so he could see my expression.

"Yeah. Do you know him?"

His brow furrowed. "Yeah, I know him. Don't tell me, you think he's attractive."

I stayed silent for a moment, studying his face. My mouth twitched up a little as I cracked a smile. Pulling him back to me I kissed him again, this time with more passion and force. I wanted him, not just physically. I wanted him to want *me*. My relationship experiences were limited to say the least, and more than anything I wanted someone to reciprocate the insane lust and need that I felt in my strange little head.

"No, actually. Sure, he may be pretty but he's not my type." We were separated by mere inches when I spoke. "He wants me to find some stripper who ghosted him."

Eric chuckled. "Does Daddy know?"

"No. And he won't, unless things get fucky."

"Are you sure that's wise? Pissing off Liam...."

I sighed loudly. "It's not going to piss off Liam. This girl ghosted him for a reason. When we find out for sure that he got played, he will run away with his tail between his legs, and we'll never hear from him again."

"So where do we go looking for this girl?"

"Ren, apparently. Are you down to go today?"

"Are you worried about running into Bliss?"

I shrugged. "Should I be?"

"I wouldn't. You made your point the last time you saw them." He leaned in and kissed my cheek, nuzzling his face into my neck. My heart hurt a bit thinking about the last time I saw my former friend; there'd been a showdown with her and her vampire buddies after they kidnapped one of my tech's and blew up her lab at the university. In the fight with Bliss, I forced a demon, the demon that formed when my prophecy got thrown off course, into her body. No one knew, not even Eric.

You should rephrase that. You didn't force anything. You didn't stop it, but you didn't make it happen. I think we can call that plausible deniability, don't you?

Pulling away from him I looked deep in his eyes. If he found out the truth, he would reject me for sure, but it would be better if I just told him instead of him discovering the truth.

"What's wrong?" He asked.

I smiled, kissing him softly on the lips. I felt my hands

tingling. "Nothing."

Spending the better part of the day looking into this 'Meg', I wasn't surprised when I came up with nothing. Close to the end of the day I left my office and went to the end of the hall to knock on Chris Lewis's door.

My Uncle Ted's partner and the L in L&B Investigations, Chris Lewis could be referred to as a man of many talents. One of them is keeping shit in line for the owners of Ren. He would be able to tell me something about Meg, and what I would be getting myself into walking back into Ren.

"Come in," he called through the door after I knocked.

I smiled and waved as I put my head in the door. "Got a sec?"

He motioned for me to come in and sit down, not looking up from his laptop.

"Can you tell me anything about a stripper named Meg that works at Ren?" I asked.

He stopped for a moment, his eyes turning to the ceiling. "Long white blonde hair?"

"That's the one. Is she there tonight?"

He looked back at his laptop, and I heard him clicking through some files. "Yep, she should be. Why?"

"I need to ask her some questions about a case I am working on."

He looked out from behind his laptop. "Do I need to know?"

"Nope. It's nothing super serious."

"Alright. Just a head's up, she's feisty. She'll probably give you a hard time."

I sighed loudly. "Great. Have you seen Bliss lately? Or the Kinkaid's?"

He looked up at the ceiling again, clearly trying to remember. I could feel the tension in my stomach, knotting up in anticipation.

"I haven't seen the Kinkaid's in a while, and Bliss is there every night. But I wouldn't be concerned, her and Meg hate each other so she won't come around if you're talking to her." He clearly knew that Bliss and I were no longer friends, which I assumed my uncle covered. They knew nothing about my prophecy, my new title, magic, or supernatural craziness.

"Good to know. Thanks for the tip." I got up and started for the door.

"And Camille?" He called back to me without looking up from his laptop.

"Yeah, boss man?"

"Don't do anything stupid."

I saluted him before closing the door behind me.

Eric and I finished up our day and headed out. We decided we were going to stop by Ren early in an attempt to talk to Meg before she started her night, then go grab some dinner when we were done. We ended up outside Ren before it got dark.

Eric turned to me as I stood outside the front door of the club, staring at the neon sign. "Are you good, Cas?"

"Yeah. Yeah, I'm good. Let's do this." Smiling brightly, I pushed open the door and we headed inside.

Tor the bartender stocked the bar when we approached; she smiled at me when she saw me. "Hey girlie! Surprised to see you."

"Hey Tor! Is Meg around?" I kept my smile as big as I could while trying not to seem like I faked it.

"Yeah, she's in the back. You know where the lockers are, right? You can head back, but your dude will have to stay out here." She gestured towards Eric, who stood a few feet away from me.

"That's not a problem. Thanks Tor." I smiled then turned to Eric. "Go find a seat, I won't be long."

He looked at me awkwardly, staring around the room. "Any advice on where? I've never been here before."

I pointed to a table off to the side in the dark, with a view of the stage but where he wouldn't be easily spotted. "You'll be safe there. Call me if anything happens."

He kissed me on the cheek then went and sat down, immediately taking out his phone.

Walking past the far end of the bar, I headed through the door to the lockers. I only went back there once or twice, my brief stint as a waitress to help out Chris Lewis didn't last long. During that time, I hadn't seen hardly any of the strippers, mind you I probably couldn't tell the difference at the time.

Walking into the room, a woman stood in front of a locker slightly turned away from me. Her long white blonde hair cascaded down her back, barely touching her naked body; her creamy pale skin looked blemish free and flawless.

"Excuse me? Meg?" I stopped about a foot away from her, trying not to seem too assuming. My hands started to tingle, and I knew golden boy wasn't as good as he thought. She turned around, her pupils dilated as she looked me up and down.

"Yes. Do I know you?" She asked sweetly.

"No, I don't think so. My name is Camille Bishop, I'm a private investigator." Her smile grew wider when I said my name. "You made quite an impression on a young man, and he sent me looking for you."

She laughed. "Honey, making an impression on men is my job. You'll have to be more specific than that."

"His name is Lorcan Fitzpatrick."

This time she laughed harder, tilting her head back and shaking her hair as she did. "Oh, the royal wolf himself?"

"Excuse me?"

"Let's not play coy, Camille. Can I call you Camille? I know who you are. I knew the second you walked into the building." She grabbed a bottle of coconut smelling lotion and began to smooth it onto her bare skin. It felt very strange having a conversation like this with a completely naked woman.

"He thinks you're human." I said.

"Do you?"

I stared at her and thought for a minute, trying to assess what sort of feeling I got from her. "No. But you are

something I have not encountered yet. My experience is....
limited."

"That's quite alright. And why is the little wolf lordling
looking for me?"

"Because he thinks you had a real connection. He says
he genuinely cares for you."

She put her hand on her hip, leaning slightly to the
side, standing perfectly in her enormous stripper heels. She
reminded me of the cartoon character Jessica Rabbit from
that movie Who Framed Roger Rabbit, all exaggerated
curves and full lips.

"He doesn't know what he's talking about." She stated.
"I hear stuff like that all the time, but if they knew the *real*
me, they wouldn't want to be with me."

"He seemed pretty genuine."

"He doesn't even know what I am, Camille."

"So, enlighten him. Give him the chance to prove
himself."

"Even if I did, I am not a werewolf. He has to marry
someone who would help the pack."

I smiled. "Who said anything about marrying him?
There is a whole lot of shit in between random hookup and
marrying someone. Pick one of those and see where it goes."

"I think I like you."

"I think I like you too. Can you do me a solid and keep
an eye on Bliss Fiori and the Kinkaid's when they are here?
I need a general idea of what they are doing."

"I would prefer not to be involved with anything
associated with...." she shivered a little. "Bliss Fiori."

"Ok, well," I took a business card out of my purse and handed it to her. "Here's my number. Let's have coffee or something. Then we can discuss what you want to do about Lorcan. If you don't want to see him, maybe we'll make a video or something. But we shouldn't do that when you're.... naked."

She laughed. "I agree. Thanks for understanding."

"Anytime." I smiled and nodded, turning to head out the door. "If you don't call me, I am going to come back looking for you. So... call me."

Back in the main room, I noticed a tall female looking figure leaning over to talk to Eric. From this far away I couldn't get a good look at her, but the hair on the back of my neck stood up.

Rushing over, the lime green bra and panty set became more visible. Bliss turned and smiled at me when I approached, but the eyes were not *her* eyes. Looked like her demon house guest took over priority. Hopefully Eric didn't notice.

He looked up at me; his eyes were glazed over like he got wasted in my absence. He blinked a few times and it disappeared, back to his normal self.

"Ready to go?" I asked him, holding out my hand.

"Absolutely." He grabbed on and I pulled him up. Bliss looked oddly at us both, her head tilting to one side.

"Can I help you?" I asked her.

It. Whatever you'd want to call *it.*

A maniacal smile curled up across her face, her eyes

wide. "No. You already did. Thank you."

"Whatever. Let's go." Linking arms with Eric, I pulled him out of Ren and back onto the street.

3.

"Well, that was weird." Eric shook his head a few times when we stepped out on the sidewalk. The sun just went down, and in typical Canadian fashion the weather became really windy and cold. Grabbing his arm, I dragged him down the street towards his car as he stumbled around for a few minutes. We parked in the pay parking lot a short distance away, the cost outweighing the hefty ticket if we'd parked on the street by the front door.

"Sorry. She's fucked up." I pulled him closer to me for warmth. "I think Tobias is giving her drugs. Did she do any weird *bruja* shit to you?"

"I don't think so." He kissed my hand. "But I'm starving. Let's go get something to eat."

We quickly got back to his car and got moving. I tried to fix my hair in the tiny mirror and make myself look presentable.

"What's wrong?" He glanced at me a few times as I

futzed.

"Well, I met Meg." I brushed my faded purple hair out of my face. "And standing next to a goddess like that, I feel like a golem." I hesitated. "She knew what I was, and that Lorcan was the wolf heir. But he doesn't know what she is. He actually thinks she's human."

"There isn't a long list of possibilities of what she is. Did you ask her?"

"Indirectly. And she wouldn't tell me yet. But I gave her my number, told her to call me so we can chat. If she doesn't want to actually see Lorcan in person again, I'll get her to make a video." I smiled at my reflection. "I totally get why he's all fucky for her. She's really hot. And not just hot, like sexy seductive...."

Eric laughed. "Oh, I know exactly what she is."

"What do you mean?"

"Unless you randomly started swinging both ways, she's definitely used her powers on you. My guess is she's a succubus. If she could hide it from Lorcan, she's probably very powerful."

"She's a what?"

"A succubus. A demon that feeds off of sexual energy." He shivered slightly. "I have a serious craving for bacon. What can we get that has bacon?"

"How would Lorcan not know that? Is he not powerful himself as the heir to the pack? Isn't that kind of important to exert dominance or some shit?"

He chuckled. "The golden boy can fight, but in terms of power it works differently for shifters than it does for people like us."

"People like us, huh?" I smiled, leaning over the centre console and licking the tip of his earlobe.

"We need to get some meat first. With bacon. Lots of bacon."

After a brief search we found a Burger King, and I spent the better part of an hour watching him scarf down a Baconator. Then another.

"So 'people like us'?" I bit the tip off a French fry.

"Are you going to tell me what happened with Jesse?" he asked.

"Millie should mind her business."

"She's worried you are going to do something stupid."

I smiled and batted my eyelashes. "Who me? Never!"

"So, tell me you didn't summon Lilly Darling as soon as you got off the phone with Millie." He wiped his face with his napkin while I scowled at him. "I know you, Cas. You can't fool me."

"It's just a failsafe. I heard her when she talked about karma."

"What did he do?"

My vision blurred as my eyes filled with tears. "He got another girl pregnant when he was with me, and rather than do the right thing he abandoned them. He abandoned a child so he could continue to treat me like shit."

"Is that the part that bothers you? The abandoning?"

"Yes." I wiped my tears with the back of my hand. "If he had left me to care for the kid, or at least told me so he could be part of the kid's life he would just be a shitty boyfriend. But abandoning the kid entirely? That's a dick move. He's a shitty person. There is no denying once you know he did that. How did I not know that?"

Eric said nothing, looking down at the greasy paper where his burger once sat and saying, "Wasn't enough. Need more."

"Are you good? This is so unlike you."

He smiled. "Fine. Just hungry."

He left the table without another word, heading back to the cashier. I gathered up our things, told him to get the order to go, took his keys and headed outside.

"Sorry. I just can't sit in there anymore." I told him when he arrived. He put his sack of fast food in the back.

"And I am sorry that 90% of our conversations revolve around the fuckery that is my life." My eyes turned away from him, watching the dark shapes move by as we drove.

He shrugged. "All part of growing up, I guess."

"What the fuck is that supposed to mean?"

"Nothing." He sighed. "Absolutely nothing."

"Stop the car. I'll take the bus home."

"No, don't be like that. I'm sorry, ok? I didn't mean it." He put his hand on my knee. I tried to smile, looking at him quickly. Our eyes met briefly, and then a bright light flashed in the windshield.

4.

It all happened so fast.

Light flashed in the car, then something slammed into its side, and we were spinning. Eric put one hand defensively across my body while gripping the wheel with the other. Once, twice, three times before we came to a halt, then complete silence for what seemed like an eternity.

My neck throbbed. So much that my eyes were watering, and when I turned to Eric, he looked horrified.

"Oh my God, are you OK?" He held out a hand, careful of where he touched me.

"I think so. My neck really hurts though." A tap on his window made us both jump. Figures loomed outside, headlights masking their identity.

Eric touched my cheek. "Stay here. I am going to go talk to this dude."

"You don't need my help?"

He leaned over and kissed me. "If I do, I will get you.

I promise."

Pain thumped behind my ear and down through my shoulder. Itchy little pinpoints made my hands tingle, like waves of electricity shooting through my skin.

The flashing red and white lights were comforting; I moved to open my passenger door and got hit by a wave of gut ripping nausea.

The door suddenly opened and luckily the person dodged out of the way seconds before I leaned out the door and threw up all over the sidewalk.

Strong arms reached in and pulled me out of the vehicle. The world began to swim.

My vision became blurry than faded to black.

5.

My memories of the hours following the accident are hazy. My mind didn't completely clear until I woke up in my bed, the pain in my neck glazed over but still there. With no neck brace in sight a big prescription bottle stood sentry on my bedside table. My hands itched like they'd been bit by ten thousand mosquitoes. Sandpaper felt like it coated my mouth. I moved to get up, that haze turning into a dull ache that forced me back down.

"Hello!" I called out weakly, my voice cracking like a prepubescent boy. I felt helpless and I fucking hated it.

The door opened and closed, and I felt a presence beside my bed. Trying to turn my head the pain exploded, Eric's face splotched out in white as the pain eased.

"Hey," he smiled at me as I reached out for him.

"Can you heal me?" I asked. "I need something to drink."

"I'm sorry. My healing seems to be out of juice or something at the moment." He gently stroked the top of my head.

I reached up to swat at him. "Drink. Water. Agua. Bullshit later."

He chuckled softly, helping me into a sitting position. He produced a water bottle, seemingly out of his ass, and handed it to me.

I guzzled back half, then gestured to the bottle of pills. "What are those?"

"Percocet."

"Bitchin. Gimme three."

"Cas."

I huffed. "Am I allowed? I am in pain. What the hell happened?"

"We were in a car accident. I got sideswiped. We spun, I'm confident that's how you hurt your neck. Doctor thinks you may have whiplash. You exhibited some concussion symptoms, so we are watching you closely."

"Ted's ok?"

He laughed out loud this time. "I'm under strict guidelines. The cat's out of the bag about our relationship by the way."

I shrugged. "That's fine. Where are we on the pain meds?"

"I'm sorry. This is all my fault. You are in pain…."

"So stop squawking and heal me. Boom. All good."

He grabbed the bottle and shook two pills into his palm, passing them to me with the bottle of water. I quickly swallowed them, handing the water bottle over and sliding down till I lay flat.

"Will you lay here with me for a while?" I grabbed his hand and interlaced his fingers with mine. "Don't know what Ted's rules are and I don't care at the moment."

"They apply to other things, so don't worry." He stretched out beside me, curling his body around so we were spooning. As his arm settled around my waist, I wanted him to touch me more.

You silly shit. You're injured and drugged, and your biggest concern is humpy time?

He kissed the back of my neck, then slowly down my shoulder. Visions of the hand that currently circled my waist moving lower, exploring, made me smile. That bit of calm put me so at ease I closed my eyes, sleep quickly catching up with me.

6.

He stayed. Even during my restless sleep, the medicated haze pulling me in and out as I winced in pain. My magic liked him; sensing his presence, it crept along my edges, trying to get closer to him.

Leaning in, I breathed deeply and took in his scent. He must have felt me stirring, because he leaned over and kissed my shoulder.

"Good morning." His warm breath on my neck gave me goose bumps. "How are you feeling?"

"Honestly? Like I would rather be having this conversation naked."

His lips touched the space where my neck connected to my shoulder. "Soon."

"You say that a lot. I am starting to wonder if you're not really attracted to me."

"What kind of man would I be if I did that while you were injured?"

I chuckled. "That's what I thought you would say."

"Would it make you feel better if we did it right now?" His hand began to slowly move down my stomach.

"I don't need a pity fuck." My eyelids grew heavy, harder to keep open. "I just want to feel wanted. Like someone really cares."

He kissed the back of my neck and I felt warmth spread from his hand throughout my body.

I giggled to myself. "That's cheating."

"You are one of the most frustrating human beings I have ever met." His lips softly touched the back of my earlobe. "But I love you so much I don't have the words."

7.

I'd never been one for drugs.

Living with an addict, drugs lose their allure. Sure, I experimented a little but nothing note worthy.

But when I opened my eyes the next day, I enjoyed the comfortably numb feeling that flowed through my body and brain. For the first time, as my eyes adjusted to the light coming in the window, I *got* it.

Perfect. You're already a hot mess. Now you're a drug addict?

SHUT UP BRAIN.

Eric slept quietly beside me. I turned to face him, wincing in pain as I shifted positions. The movement caused him to stir, and he opened one eye and smiled.

"Good morning." He leaned over and kissed me softly.

"Morning. What time is it? We better motor or we'll be late for work."

"He gave us the day off."

"Oh." I smiled. "Did you see them this morning?"

"Yeah. Ted, Cuddy and Maritza."

I groaned. "Glad I missed them playing happy family."

"She seems like a nice girl."

"She's a plant from Bliss's coven." *Shit.* "They think I did something to Bliss and are watching me until they figure out what it is."

"How come you never told me?"

"Because it's stupid. They're blaming me instead of facing the fact that their homegirl is a vampire puppet. Maritza claims to actually like Cuddy though." I pulled myself closer and kissed him. "But now that we're alone."

"Do you want me to heal you?"

No more pain meant no more drugs. "No. Not yet."

We silently stared into each other's eyes for a few minutes. As I leaned in to kiss him both our phones started beeping.

"Saved by the bell." He started to speak but I shushed him as I reached for my nightstand.

Multiple messages from Millie flashed on my screen. Eric must have informed her, by the contents of the message it sounded like she and Nya prepared some healing.

"Millie and Nya got some witchy healing shit for us." I grumbled. "But I'm fine. Just give me two Percocet's and I'll be good."

"Cas...." His eyes narrowed.

"If I didn't know you guys this is how I would have to deal with pain from an accident. It's not that bad. Keep that in mind."

He leaned down, cradling the back of my head with his

hand and kissing me. I felt warmth spread out of his hand into my head and neck, which after a few moments fizzled out and stopped. Eric pulled away, paused, and set my head back down.

"That was weird." He said flatly. The look in his eyes made me think that the healing from Millie wasn't entirely for me. He handed me two pills and a water bottle, which I happily took.

"Help me up. I'll have a quick shower and we'll go to Millie's. Ok?" I took his hand in mine, smiling calmly at him.

He nodded, not looking directly at me.

"Wanna join me?" I asked as he helped me sit up. Once I was vertical everything felt different, the aftereffects of the pain tablets leaving everything in a coated haze.

"I do but I don't want to hurt you." He smiled at me when we both stood.

"You won't." I pulled my shirt off over my head in one quick motion, ignoring the sharp pain that shot through my shoulder into the side of my neck. His warm hands felt good as they touched my body.

Before I could say anything, he took his shirt off, my hands immediately went to his skin and the lines of the muscles in his stomach. He pulled me to him and kissed me, my nipples hardened when his chest touched mine. His strong arms went around me, and he eased me back onto my bed and crawled on top.

We continued to kiss as we fumbled with each other's pants, quickly deciding to pause and remove them ourselves.

I struggled with mine, and once his came off he helped with mine and we were finally naked next to each other.

This felt like a big moment, a moment that seemed a long time in the making. I suddenly got nervous, worried that this could make or break our relationship. He was older and more experienced; I hoped I could measure up.

Eric ran his hand up my side, cupping my breast and slowly rubbing the pad of his thumb on my nipple. I moved to reciprocate, trying to touch him and he eased me back down, moving on top of me so I could only reach his neck and his chest. His exploring hands continued to move down, and I gasped when his fingers found their way between my legs.

"Are you ok?" He paused, looking down at me.

"It's been a while. Sorry." I pulled him back down to kissing me; he chuckled as his fingers slowly began to play with my intimate parts. He knew exactly where to touch, to push, to stroke, his fingers moving in what seemed like a well choreographed dance that drove me wild. Soon I writhed underneath him, moving my hips in an upward motion in an attempt to meet his hardness. What I could feel drove me wilder, his hardness the largest I ever came in contact with.

"Now. Please." I whispered between kisses. He reached up behind my head and pulled a condom out from under the pillow.

I laughed. "So, you were prepared?"

"Didn't want to ruin the moment." He tore open the wrapper with his teeth, and then handed it to me. I smiled, and he kissed slowly down my neck and licked my earlobe as I took him in my hand and rolled the condom on.

He most definitely won in the size contest.

"You're sure you're ok?" He asked again, his hot breath on my neck giving me goose bumps.

I nodded in agreement, letting out a loud moan when he entered me.

I felt his toes curl and his fingers clench as he began moving back and forth, in and out inside me. I met his every move, my hips thrusting forward and upward. My hands wrapped around his neck, and he moaned as he kissed me again.

As he began to speed up, I lost myself in the feelings, I felt myself opening up to him and connecting to him in a way that I'd never done with another human being. My magic liked him, it reached out to his and they began to intertwine in their own euphoric dance as our bodies moved. Soon the orgasms hit me like a wave, and one after the other my body erupted as my hips met his. Something about the magic sent us to this other place where we were more connected, and I could tell he was riding it like I was. We held each other tight, kissing as Eric climaxed with one last hard push inside me.

We both paused for a moment, trying to catch our breath as the sensations in our bodies slowed down. He went to move, and as he did it sent a wave of pleasure through me, so I pulled him back.

"Not yet." I said quietly. He kissed me, a soft sweaty kiss that I would argue to be one of the best we'd ever had.

He kissed my cheek and nuzzled up to my neck.

"I'm sorry we waited so long." He said to me.

"It was totally worth the wait." I chuckled. He kissed me again on the soft skin below my ear.

After a few minutes he got up, being sure to remove the condom and put it in my waste basket. He lay back down beside me, and we lay in each other's arms, naked on top of my blankets. I didn't usually like being so exposed, but with Eric it was ok. I didn't mind him seeing me this way.

He held me, stroking my hair gently, and I felt truly normal. It was supposed to be like this, and all that nonsense that happened with Jesse was bullshit. I almost wanted to summon him again so he could see, so he would know that I will be happy without him, and in spite of him.

"They'll start calling." Eric said after a few minutes.

"Who?"

"Millie. The others. If they don't hear from us, they'll start calling."

"So, let's tell them to fuck off and stay in bed. Or better yet, I'll pack a bag and go to your house, so we don't have to wear clothes at all." He laughed, kissing my cheek as I spoke. "How are we going to get there anyhow? Your car got smashed."

"I have a rental till it's fixed." He replied.

"Awesome. While that sounds amazing, I think we need to go get healed. Both of us." He crawled down the bed and stood, moving around the side to help me up. "But a shower would be amazing."

We showered together, and while there was lots of kissing and touching, we didn't do it again. I couldn't stop looking at his amazing body.

He helped me get dressed, which proved oddly intimate. Once we were both done, he smiled strangely at me.

"You want to pack a bag?" He asked with a big grin on his face.

I tried to hide my excitement, shrugging my shoulders only to flinch in pain. "Yeah, ok. I guess so."

He laughed again and pulled me in for a kiss.

We didn't talk much on the way to Millie's, but we were constantly touching, his hands were warm and made me feel strong. I noticed some thin strands of white weaving up that hand as if my magic wanted to touch him too. The rental smelt oddly like disinfectant.

Part of me wanted to ask him, was I, no *it*, good enough. Would this just be a flash in the pan, and he didn't feel like I did?

Foolish girl. That magic orgasm you all had was real. Unless that's common for him, you're good.

We parked out front of Millie's; I saw a car parked in the driveway that I didn't recognize behind Millie's SUV.

"Someone else is here?" I asked Eric, he looked as confused as I was.

"I guess we'll find out." He kissed my knuckles and we got out.

Millie looked happier than I'd ever seen her when she

answered the door.

"Hey! I am so happy you guys are here! There is someone I would like you to meet." She ushered us inside, and I held tight on Eric's hand like a small child grappling on a security blanket.

A man in his early 20's sat at the table drinking wine with Nya. He looked short even though he sat, stocky and muscular. When he looked up and smiled, I saw Nya's face and my tension eased.

"Camille, Eric, this is my son Ledo." Millie placed a hand on her son's shoulder. "Ledo, this is…."

"The *blanchmains* and the Merlin." He stood just below my eye level which made him short for a guy. "Nice to meet you both. I have heard a lot about you."

"When we told Ledo that you guys had been looking into Excalibur he wanted to help." Millie pulled us both out chairs, offering glasses of wine before sitting back down. She smiled; her face slightly pink with the warm glow of coming drunkenness.

Nya leaned forward. "My brother is a relic hunter." She giggled.

Eric let go of my hand when he sat, motioning to me if I wanted wine that I refused. Mixing that with pain meds was a road I was not prepared to take just yet.

"What's your interest in Excalibur?" I asked Ledo.

He laughed. "Who isn't interested in Excalibur?"

"The sword is supposed to possess great power. That's why I assume everyone wants it."

"Is that why you want it?"

"As a descendant of the lady of the lake, I feel like it's my birthright to protect it until the one who is supposed to wield it shows up."

Ledo smiled again. "I'm a descendant too, remember?"

I took out my arm, rolled up my sleeve and extended my white hand to him. His eyes widened, and he reached out and poked the white part of my skin with his finger.

"I think I have a bit more of a stake in this, don't you agree?" I smiled this time and he eased back, knowing he would not win the argument.

"What do you know about these immortal old ones?" I asked.

"Not a lot. Some think they're a myth. Some say that technically anyone over 500 years old should be considered an old one. Why?"

I looked at Millie. "You didn't tell him?"

"Tell me what?" Ledo looked quickly from me to his mother.

"I met Dr. Frankenstein. Came into my office and everything. Calls himself Dr. Croft. He works for the Kinkaid's. We had a little…. issue with his granddaughter."

Ledo raised his eyebrows. "Issue?"

"Long story."

Ledo eased back in his seat, a big grin on his face. "I have a feeling you and I are going to get along *real* well."

"So! You all need some healing!" Millie clapped her hands together.

"I'm good. Percocet's got it handled." I leaned back and grinned.

"Easy there," Eric put a hand on my shoulder, "I think a little would be helpful."

"Alright, alright." I waved them on, and Millie and Nya got up and began going around the room gathering different things. "I'd be more worried about his powers being on the fritz."

I turned my chair so I could watch as Millie and Nya went to work making what I thought to be a potion. They took down various vials and jars from a shelf that covered one of Millie's dining room walls, gathering bunches of dried herbs that lay out on a countertop.

The haze of the medicine softened the world around me, with Eric and I finally having sex my world glittered and sparkled and I smiled like a dope filled idiot. Punch drunk and floating, Millie watched me with a confused expression.

"I'm fine. I am used to recovering in non magical ways. Focus on him. Please." I smiled and nodded at her, trying not to look her too closely in the eye.

After everything I went through am I not entitled to enjoy some moments?

My attention turned to Eric's hand as it hangs at his side, the rest of them continue on around me as I stare mindlessly at him. The negative thoughts that plague my psyche have actually backed off for the moment, so I am not constantly worried about how sex changes everything.

Or am I?

Millie said something to me, and I don't hear her at first. "Pardon me?" I asked.

"Great. Now that Cas's all zonked out on pain meds, we

have to figure out what to do about her demon without her." Millie huffed in frustration.

"*My* demon? You want to shit on anyone about that I will summon my Moms right now." I pointed at her.

"One of Bliss's coven is cozying up to Ted's son Christian until they figure out what's wrong with Bliss." Eric told her and I growled at him.

"You don't think that's worth mentioning?" Millie exclaimed.

I shook my head. "No. I told that girl straight that Bliss is a snake and about the Kinkaid shit. And that if she fucked with Cuddy I will destroy her." I said the last in a sing song voice, being sure to wink at the end.

"Oh! And I did this!" I held up my hand, eyed a blade from across the room and it shook before it flew off the table and into my hand, where I slammed it into the tabletop blade first. It stood on end when I released it. Everyone jumped, especially Ledo, and I laughed as Eric pulled the blade out of the wood.

"It was much scarier in my kitchen." I tried to reassure them.

Millie rolled her eyes. "We will have to work on your intimidation tactics." She handed us both several small vials. "It's going to take a few doses. But they should help."

I gave her thumbs up before turning back to Ledo. "Have you ever been to an auction?"

"Plenty. Why?"

"Well, my dad had these insanely detailed files about items the Kinkaid's acquired and this buyer that would get things for them. No clear picture or anything of who he or she is, no name just a string of aliases. I want to go to an auction and see if I can find this person, and they may be the first lead to find the sword." I poured a little wine for myself and took a sip, my mouth felt dry. "I have a file on who had it, but it was stolen from them, I am assuming, by the same person who is buying things from the auctions."

"Why would you think that?"

"Call it my Spidey sense." Or that my dad believed it, so I went with it. He'd also written out a physical description of two tall, beautiful but imposing women who he saw at multiple auctions that seemed suspicious. But I would keep that info close to the chest.

"Did they," Ledo gestured to his mom and sister, "tell you nothing about me?"

I shook my head. "Nope."

Nya laughed and rolled her eyes. "He's trying to figure out how to break our dad's curse."

"It's more complicated than that. I'm a relic hunter by trade." He sat up a little straighter, adjusting the sleeves of his plaid over shirt. "I could probably answer a lot of your questions. Any chance I could peek at your dad's files?"

"Nope." I drank one of the vials. It tasted herbal and medicinal, felt warm going down my throat into my stomach. As it made its way down my esophagus it moved through to the ache in my neck and took root.

I smiled to myself, my eyelids getting heavy. My power crept up my arm, angry at the intrusion of this strange brew, and a stinging sensation began to tingle from the back of my head down my shoulders.

"Ruh roh." I groaned as I rolled my shoulders around.

"What's the problem?" Millie asked.

"What did you put in that thing?" I rubbed my hand across the back of my neck. "My power *does not like it at all.*"

Eric stood and came towards me, putting his hand on the back of my neck. Sensing his presence my power moved in his direction but remained tethered to the pain spot.

"That's odd." Eric said. "I can feel something moving under her skin. Can the potion hurt her at all?"

"No." Millie and Nya said in unison.

I touched his hand on my neck. "No, it's cool. I'm good."

I felt something when our hands met in that spot, a piece of dark that sat on the edge of him. I wanted to pick at it. I wanted to scratch that *thing* and see if it bled.

"So, I am going to an auction tomorrow afternoon. You all want to tag along?"

I smiled, leaning forward and smiling. "Absolutely."

Ledo spent the rest of the evening filling us in about this auction the next day. An item in the auction catalogue fit most of the description of an item he was looking for; he insisted he needed to see it in person to confirm.

Eric helped me back into the car, eyeing me curiously. Exhaustion crept over me, and I tried to fight it. After what happened earlier, I *so* badly wanted to go back to his place and spend a naked night in bed, but with how I currently felt that probably wouldn't happen.

As he drove, I began to doze off. The rhythmic sound of the engine and the bump and thump of the tires on the road were soothing, I tried my best to fight it but soon enough I drifted off.

8.

The next time I opened my eyes I lay flat on a bed that wasn't mine. Eric's smell wrapped around me, and when my eyes adjusted, I saw his back rising and falling beside me.

His bed felt soft and comfortable. I could feel nothing, which I hoped meant that dumb healing potion worked. I reached out for Eric, his skin so inviting. Slithering closer to him I curled myself around his body and quickly drifted off to sleep.

The next time I opened my eyes I felt his presence behind me, the soft tip of his finger ran along the back of my neck and down my shoulder. He kissed me softly in the same spot, my toes curled in udder bliss.

"Good morning." He said softly in my ear. I loved the feel of his breath on my neck.

"Morning." I replied, raising my hand so I could touch his cheek.

"I like you being here in the morning." His arms felt good around my waist. "I'm sorry we didn't do this sooner."

I chuckled. "Me too."

"I'm making bacon for breakfast."

"Just bacon? That's a little weird."

"No of course not. But what do you have against bacon?"

"Nothing. I just think it's odd that you have been so interested in pork lately."

He shrugged, leaning in and kissing me again. "Are you ready for today?"

"Fuck! What time is it? I have to call Ted."

"Already done. I told him we will be out of the office today working on your new case. Lorcan Fitzpatrick is on the books and all."

"But the auction has…."

"No, but you got a call from an unknown number last night. Could be your girl." He chuckled. "So, we could meet her after the auction."

I turned around so I could see him, pulling him close and kissing his lips. Pain and stiffness made me flinch, and he pulled away and looked me in the eyes.

"You ok?" He asked.

I groaned. "I'm sore. I don't know if I am going to take another one of those healing potions."

"Gimme another day and I should be back to normal."

"Are you sure? If you need time, then take some. I don't know how any of this shit works. I wouldn't want you to hurt yourself when I can heal just like a normal person would."

The corners of his mouth upturned slightly in a smile. "A normal person?"

"Shhh. I can pretend."

He kissed me and I closed my eyes.

We showered together, and he cooked food while I attempted to make myself look presentable.

Looking at my face in his mirror, it seemed different. A pinkish glow lit up my cheek bones, and my eyes sparkled in a way they hadn't before.

Could this be what happy feels like?

Eric made us both omelette's that were amazing, with an insane amount of bacon on the side. I thought women only got cravings like that, it seemed a little excessive.

"You magic pregnant or something?" I asked him between bites.

He sputtered out a laugh. "That's a weird question."

"Once again, I have no idea how this shit works. And you are eating bacon like you're eating for two."

He shrugged, smiling at me as he popped another strip of delicious fried pork into his mouth. Before he could reply my phone started to beep, Ledo letting us know that he would meet us downtown at the auction house. He also texted a barcode we could use as a parking pass, something I'd not even thought of. Not being the one that drives it never crossed my mind.

We hadn't packed my laptop so I got Eric to bring his, not that our phones couldn't do most of the same things, but I wanted something with more juice for emergencies.

The truth of the matter being that a phone could never fully replace a computer, no matter how advanced the tech got, because of size alone.

But I'm sure one day they'll invent a phone that's screen can expand to 16 inches. They may have already, and I am just behind.

We drove to one of the posher parts of downtown Toronto, the parking attendant scanned the barcode Ledo sent, and we were able to park in the underground for free. Ledo met us just outside the entrance. Wearing a navy blazer and khaki's, he looked smart and professional. He chuckled at Eric and me, in our usual business casual clothes we wear to work. He seemed surprised to see Eric in a sweater with a bird on it, the same one he wore the day we first met.

"I'm happy we didn't have to have a conversation about wardrobe." Ledo shook both our hands.

"Of course not. We are professionals, you know." I poked him in the ribs as we went inside.

9.

A mixed group of people made up the crowd, from older couples in their furs and pearls, to a bunch of younger folks in suits that cost more than I make in a month. I bit back the urge to growl at them when they walked past me.

"Are lots of these people like you?" I asked Ledo.

His eyebrow rose. "What do you mean 'like me'?"

"Relic hunters. Bounty hunters. I must admit I am fascinated by what you do."

"A few. Lots of them are interns at bigger galleries and museums looking to pick stuff up on the cheap." He found us three seats in the back corner with a good view of the room. I perched on the edge of my seat and scanned the crowd.

"She's here." Ledo said, his voice soft. I turned and spotted who'd got his attention; a tall, copper haired woman in a tan trench coat and big sunglasses and her blonde companion, equally as tall with hair that cascaded down her back. The blonde's skin looked pale, but naturally so, where the copper haired one's olive skin glowed with warmth.

Ledo couldn't stop staring at them; I discretely took a few photos of them both. Neither of them removed their large black sunglasses. Something about the way they moved, tall, elegant and with determination made me think they were both regal. Two of the finest examples of women most would ever come in contact with.

"Who's the chick?" I asked him.

"I don't know. But they're both so gorgeous it's like they're...." He paused, stopping himself and shaking his head.

"So what item are we looking for?" Eric asked.

"Supposedly there is a women's mirrored compact from the 1950's on the block. Someone inlayed it with a magical stone, and now the mirror inside traps ghosts in it. If someone figures out how to get them out, it's potentially really dangerous." Ledo tried to keep his eyes in front of him, but on occasion I noticed he and Eric glancing over at the two mystery women.

Just as the auctioneer approached the podium, three more women walked in. Different than the previous two, they were much shorter and dressed in all black. All three looked exquisite with their hair woven into intricate braided updos.

I took their picture as well. Something about them seemed important. One of them made eye contact with me as they found a seat; dark eyes examined me and clearly did threat assessment around the room.

"What about them, Ledo?" I gestured without actually pointing.

He shrugged. "I have seen them a few times, nothing worth noting."

He motioned for me to be quiet as the auctioneer raised his hand to silence the room. Ledo and I both sat on the edge of our seats as the man spoke; something prickled up my arm and gave me goose bumps. I turned and made eye contact with Eric, he felt it too.

The auctioneer began, and I watched as he worked his way through various items like paintings and furniture. By the reactions of some of the older people in attendance I wondered if these were a deceased loved one's belongings.

"Next on the docket, a long sword of English origin with what our translator believes to be a form of ancient Welsh inscribed on the hilt. There is no known date of the making of this item, but we believe its well into the 11th century. Bidding opens at ten thousand dollars." The auctioneer gestured in very Vanna White fashion, and one of the assistants stepped forward and withdrew the large sword from its scabbard. I discreetly held up my phone and started filming; the age and the providence of this sword would appeal to the same collector who stole my sword.

Your sword?

In a flash of light, the blade sparked and became immediately inflamed, the assistant screamed in pain and dropped it as his arm caught fire. The sword burned as it fell from his hand and hit the ground.

"What the fuck is that?" I asked, filming everything.

"Could be *drnwyn*." Ledo said, looking to Eric who nodded in agreement.

"*What?!*" I threw up my free hand.

"Another mythological sword." Ledo winked at me. "Not as cool as Excalibur though."

"I need to study or some shit. I am so far behind." I shook my head, double checking my phone still filmed as they cleared the stage. The auctioneer continued the bidding, from his reaction and how quickly they cleared the fire it looked as if they were prepared for it.

While the two taller women paid close attention, the other group of three bought the flame sword for twelve thousand dollars. Taking more photos of their faces, I made an attempt to be covert.

The auctioneer moved on, and the compact Ledo mentioned appeared. The inlay possessed a reflective quality like mother of pearl and shone beautifully even in the terrible lighting. When they opened it to show the mirror, which was still intact, it flashed a strange swirl of colors. Regular people would mistake it for a trick of the light, but it made my breath catch in my throat. I pulled my sleeves down over my hands.

Bidding started at fifty dollars. With no clear maker marks or identification all they could gage the price on was materials and age. Ledo watched the crowd before bidding, with no clear interest from anyone else he picked up the item for the starting price.

"You got something to carry that in? I don't want it touching me." I told Ledo quietly.

"OK….?"

"Do you think it's a good plan for the ghost holder to

come in contact with someone who can summon ghosts who doesn't have the greatest control over her powers yet?" His eyes widened a little after I finished stating the obvious.

Ledo nodded. "I do anyways. But you have a good point."

My phone buzzed, and I ended the video so I could check the message. It was Ted, just making sure I'm alright.

Typing more than I intended I explained to him that physically I still felt sore and achy but mentally things were awesome and Eric getting me up and going today made a big difference. I thanked him for his patience and most of all his acceptance of this new thing with Eric.

Just after I hit send it buzzed again, this time from an unknown number asking if I wanted to have coffee later. Eric mentioned earlier a call from an unknown number, probably the same person.

I texted back *sure, where and when* and waited. The auction wrapped up, and we remained seated until the room cleared a bit than headed for the exit.

Before we could reach the door, someone bumped me from behind and almost knocked me down. I turned and scowled at one of the three women; her eyes seemed to glow as we made eye contact. Her warm dark brown skin looked perfectly smooth and blemish free. She scowled at first, but then I saw a click of recognition in her eyes. My magic crept up my arm into the sore spot on my neck. It felt tense, like it prepared for something to happen.

She quickly moved passed us with her friends and disappeared from sight. I mentally took note of her features, hoping it least one of the photos I took turned out.

Once we got outside, we parted ways with Ledo, he went to collect his item and we agreed to meet at Millie's later to check it out.

Back in the car I checked my messages, and the location for coffee appeared close enough for us to walk, so we decided to leave the car and go on foot. I felt pretty confident the text came from Meg because she included, *bring the Merlin if you wish.*

I showed the text to Eric. "Do you know her?"

"Not sure. I would have to see her face. There are stories about the succubus who works at Ren. No one has heard about Lorcan yet though."

"Is it really that big of a deal?"

"That the wolf pack heir fell for a succubus? To some people, yeah. To others, they would think it's cool. Some, like me, will think it's hilarious. The wolves aren't so keen on inter species mingling."

I felt myself scowling. "That's very short sighted of them."

"Not everyone is as open minded as you." He kissed me on the cheek.

After about a ten-minute walk we were at the small Café called Just Desserts. Meg sat in the window, clearly trying to soak up some of the afternoon sun on this dreary early winter day. She spotted us and smiled widely; Eric squeezed my hand.

"Promise me you won't get upset?" He began before we walked inside.

"Ruh roh."

"No. Nothing like that. But she is a succubus and could… what was the word you used? Bamboozled? She could mess with both our minds. I just want to make a pact right now if she does that to either of us, we won't get upset."

I smiled and nodded. "Of course."

10.

The first time I saw Meg I wasn't immediately suspicious, in part because I didn't know who or *what* I was dealing with. But this time when we stepped into the café, and she brushed her white blonde hair back behind her shoulder I immediately went on the defensive. She smiled a big toothy grin at us, Eric squeezed my hand.

"I am so happy you came!" She exclaimed as we sat down. She seemed much more chipper and personable then she did at Ren.

"As I mentioned, I have to tell Lorcan *something*." I smiled at the waitress, who came over and took our order for two cappuccinos.

"He could have come to Ren himself."

My eyebrows rose. "I thought he did?"

She laughed. "If he did it was on my day off."

"Well, I don't want to take up a ton of your time. How do you want to proceed?"

Meg tilted her head to one side, twisting a strand of her hair around one finger. Something about the way her skin shimmered seemed freaky and a strange thought crossed my mind.

"This isn't what you really look like. Is it?" I asked.

Eric leaned in and whispered to me. "Really powerful glamour spells."

"Can I do that too?" Meg laughed at my question; Eric smiled and nodded in reply. "That is *so* going to change stake outs!"

"For the *blanchmains* you are frighteningly uninformed." Meg took a sip of her drink.

"Oh, I have only known about my powers for like 6 weeks."

Her eyes widened a little. "Well, that does explain a few things."

"What does that mean?"

The corners of her lips turned up in a little smile. "You have no idea what you are, do you?"

I turned to Eric, a quick stab of pain up my neck made me flinch. "Why do people keep saying shit like that?"

"Because it's the truth." He whispered loud enough for Meg to hear.

"You're doing her a disservice not telling her." Meg turned her gaze to Eric.

"It's a lot to take in. I don't want to scare her."

She rolled her eyes, clicking her tongue on her teeth. She leaned towards me and said, "You have my number now. Let me know when you want to know *everything*."

"Can we get back on topic please? Lorcan. What do you want me to say to Lorcan?"

Meg sighed, glancing at Eric and smiling coyly. It took a lot of energy not to throw my coffee at her. She pulled something out of her purse, a small white envelope, and handed it to me.

"Give that to Lorcan." She looked annoyed. "See how he reacts. If he still wants to persist, text me."

I pocketed the envelope. "Thanks."

"I thought he would get the hint that I was blowing him off, but I guess not." She gathered up her stuff, stood up and put her coat on. "I hope the next time we speak it's under better circumstances."

Flipping her hair back behind her shoulder, she quickly walked out.

"That was weird." I said to Eric.

He shrugged. "Maybe when her charm didn't work, she got frustrated."

"Oh well. Hopefully Lorcan accepts whatever is in the note and we're done with it." I quickly finished my coffee. "Now, tell me about the flame sword."

About a half hour later we walked out of Just Desserts and headed back to the car. The overall vibe of downtown changed now that the workday began. Traffic died down and it almost felt peaceful. Snow began to quietly fall from the sky.

Eric reached for me, and we held hands as we walked. For just a moment I forgot all the chaos we endured and just focused on him and I being together. So caught up in my daydream I stared around without focusing and banged head on into another person.

"Shit! I'm so sorry!" I held up my arm in front of me, hunching slightly. When I looked at the person, I stumbled back a little when I came face to face with one of the girls with the braided updo from the auction.

She bore down on me like an angry dog prepared for a fight. My hands began to tingle and itch under my sleeves; my powers sent off signals throughout my body to be very careful.

Closer to her now I could see that her hair was actually finely twisted dreadlocks, the colour such a dark black I could only ever get from a bottle of dye. They were swept up in this incredible braided crown like hairstyle that accentuated her big brown eyes, her rich brown skin seemed to be glowing in irritation.

Her lips, a dark shiny burgundy colour, curled in a sneer. I lowered my gaze in deference, and she turned and walked away. As she stormed past pain shot up my neck like a stabbing needle, causing me to further hunch and lose track of any thought I'd had about that woman.

"You ok?" Eric stuck his warm hand on the back of my neck, and I cringed when he touched me, my skin suddenly felt hot and itchy.

"That was really weird." I took a few deep breaths and pulled myself back into my regular stance. "You got any painkillers left?"

He chuckled. "You know I do. You want to give the

healing spell a chance first? Use the pills as a last resort?"

"Nope." I said with a grin, standing on my tip toes and kissing the tip of his nose.

Two Percocet's and the day became entirely more pleasant. We drove to the office and after helping me inside with all my baggage, Eric disappeared. Being left on my own I felt strange.

I took a photo of the envelope and sent it to Lorcan, telling him he could collect it at any time. Beyond that my day was clear; I suspect they didn't think I would be in.

As I downloaded the photos from the auction to my laptop I heard a knock at my door, a big smile crossed my face when Q and Lemme walked in with a giant Frappuccino for me.

"What's up Bond?" Q and I fist bumped across the desk. "How are you feeling? We heard what happened, thought you could use some nectar of the Gods."

"You guys are awesome!" I took a big sip of my drink, easing back in my chair. "Did you guys come all this way just for this?"

"Naw. Boss man need's tech support." Q took a sip of her own drink. "Oh, and crazy town over here wanted to chat."

"*Bitch, I'm not crazy.*" Lemme snapped. "I know what I saw."

Lemme began digging through her bag, then pulled various sheets of paper out and spread them flat on my desk so I could see.

Q groaned loudly, calling back as she walked out, "I'll let you handle this shit show."

As soon as the door clicked shut, Lemme turned back to me. "Did you get my emails?"

"Not any recent ones. I have been a little fucky since the accident."

"Ok, well when you get a chance, I found the schematics for the lab…."

My head tilted to one side. "Lab?"

"The lab where they held me. That Nikki freak. Remember? We have to go back."

"Lemme. It's not that simple."

She stared me down like I sprouted a third eye. "Is that a joke?"

"No. We talked about this. I can't just walk in their guns blazing. I need a plan. *We* need a plan. I get that you want to rescue this person, but I am not sure you understand…"

She huffed angrily. "Oh, I understand. You made me a promise, Camille. We can't just leave her there."

I reached across my desk and took her hand. "And we won't. I promise. But you have to be prepared this is going to take some time to plan. Do you understand? These maps are very helpful."

I took every single piece of paper she laid out and got out a folder and put them inside. She still eyed me with an angry stare, surely judging to see if I told the truth or not.

"I told you I would go, and I will. It's not *if,* it's *when.*" I attempted to be forceful. This wasn't the first time Lemme sat across from me asking to storm Frankenstein's lab.

Yep, that Frankenstein. His psycho one hundred times great granddaughter kidnapped Lemme and tried to Darth Vader me. But we already know that story.

Right, Believer?

"How's school?"

She rolled her eyes at me; the udder look of distain that now formed her expression could peel a weaker person's skin off. "School is rough, Camille. My lab burnt down. I can't keep my shit straight because I can't get that chick in the tank out of my head. And what I need you to do right now is tell me you have this shit handled." Lemme moved closer, putting both her hands on the tabletop so she could lean in.

"Easy now." I said quietly, pulling back slightly. My hands began to tingle, I didn't bother moving them. When I'd rescued Lemme she'd seen them completely white.

"Have you got this shit handled, Camille?" She growled at me.

I watched her for a few minutes, staying silent, deciding on the best course of action at this moment. I cared about Q and Lemme. They were an important part of L&B Investigations; showing her a display of power, even just to scare her, would probably be a bad idea. They were also my friends. The only non magical friends I had.

What the fuck is wrong with you? Now you're talking about scaring your friend?

I allowed my power to fill the room, the energy spreading out like liquid. Lemme wouldn't fully understand but I could tell by the look on her face that she felt it. She knew the energy in the room shifted somehow.

I smiled brightly when her confused expression turned to me. "I have this handled. Thank you for the maps."

Lemme opened her mouth to say something else but before she could Q reappeared, pausing just as she walked in. "All good in the hood?"

"You bet." I said, my smile never faltering. Lemme gathered up her stuff and headed for the door.

"Thanks for the drink, guys." I smiled and waved as they both walked out without another word.

After a few minutes I opened the folder and looked over the images Lemme gave me. Sure enough they were schematics for a lab, a pretty high tech one by the looks of it. Lemme hadn't provided a plan of how to get past security though.

Lorcan texted me close to the end of the day. He didn't say much at first. I told him that it would be easier for him to come and meet with me, and he asked if I could come to the clubhouse. Before I could go to Eric's office to ask anything about it Ted popped into my doorway.

"How are you feeling?" His smile was warm and inviting.

"I'm ok. It's sore and aches but I'll be ok." I smiled back at him. "How are you?"

"I'm ok. Worried about you guys though."

"Guys?"

"You and Eric."

I sighed. I'd forgotten Ted and I hadn't spoken since he

found out about my relationship with Eric. "What are you worried about? We enjoy each other's company. He doesn't treat me like I'm defective because of all the crap that's happened recently."

"I was referring to you guys being injured but thanks, that's useful info for me to have." He chuckled. "As much as it pains me to admit it Chris did well picking Eric. He's a good guy and I like him a lot. I also like Maritza."

"Oh balls. I forgot about *Maritza.*"

"Cut that out. She's very nice and Cuddy really likes her. I won't let you ruin this for him. "He came towards the desk, leaning over and catching sight of the pictures on my laptop. He turned the screen towards him.

"What's this from?" He asked.

"The auction we went to with Millie's son this morning. Why?"

He pointed at the two women Ledo almost drooled over. "I know the blonde."

"Really? How?"

"She's a cop. Or she was a cop. Detective. Pretty high ranking too. Her name is Shae Rielle."

I grabbed a Post It and quickly wrote the name down. "Thanks Ted!"

Surprised by my excitement, he said, "You're welcome?" then turned and went back to his office.

Pushing Lorcan aside, I dove into research on Shae Rielle.

From what I could find, she still worked as a Detective. She lived in a nice condo, and her name showed up on the deed to a building in a west end neighborhood called Parkdale. About a fifteen-minute detour on the way home.

I climbed out from behind my desk and went to Eric's office. It was empty. Rather than disturb the boss men I checked my phone to see if he texted.

Nothing. Not even a courtesy text to say he fucked off to run errands. It hurt my heart a bit, and I tried to talk myself out of feeling bad. Surely it didn't mean anything.

When I got back behind my desk, I texted Eric and asked him where he went. I also texted Lorcan and asked for the address for this clubhouse.

It seemed like hours went by before I got a notification. The address wasn't far, so I packed up and headed out to the bus. Eric would have to come find me.

Public transit always felt like an adventure. I didn't have my headset so on occasion I would drift off as the bus bumped along.

About ten minutes into my trip a mother and her daughter got on the bus and sat down in front of me. Normally I wouldn't have paid attention but the two of them were surrounded by an eerie glow, like I could see their auras, which would be weird considering I didn't know what an aura was let alone if I ever saw one. The bright shiny purple hue circled them both in a protective bubble. It didn't scare me, but it created loads of questions.

When I got off the mother and I made eye contact, setting off my magical Spidey sense. She looked younger than I thought. And something in her eyes made me think she'd seen some shit.

Without thinking I smiled at her, and she smiled back.

11.

The wolf pack clubhouse happened to be down a dark back alley, closely resembling the entrance to a crappy dive bar. I gather that was by design, but it made Burnt Offerings look inviting.

I stood outside the door and scanned the vicinity looking for security cameras. Surely a notification went off when someone approached the door. When I couldn't spot anything, I pushed the small black button on the intercom just to the right of the door. It let off a standard angry beep, sounding more like someone choked a chicken than a buzzer.

After a few minutes the speaker crackled to life. "Can I help you?"

"I'm here to see Lorcan Fitzpatrick."

"Who's this?"

I sighed. "He didn't tell you I was coming? My name is Camille."

Another crackle, then a metal click by the door that I assumed meant it unlocked. I grabbed the handle and pulled, sure enough it opened.

I stepped inside the doorway to a flight of stairs going up with Lorcan standing at the top, smiling.

"You found her?" He grinned ear to ear.

"According to her you didn't try very hard." I started up the stairs to meet him, holding the handrail for support. "She said she works at Ren regularly and you would have seen her had you bothered to go in."

He rolled his eyes. "Some of the guys I met her with went and said they never saw her."

"Either you're a fool or they lied." I felt myself blush at my boldness. "Sorry. I'm just being honest."

"So, she's human, right?"

He escorted me into a large room with a pool table, a bar and some couches by a wall fireplace close to a window. Finished with black leather and dark wood, it reminded me of something from a motorcycle club hangout. We sat down in overstuffed leather chairs across from each other.

"Do you want me to be honest?" I asked.

"Absolutely."

"No. She's not human at all." I dug around in my purse until I found him the note Meg gave me, which I reluctantly handed to him. He eyed it curiously for a moment before taking it from me. Part of me kicked myself for not reading it beforehand.

"She's not? I'm surprised she could hide that from me."

"In your defense, she's *very* talented at hiding who and

what she actually is."

He eased back in the chair, flipping the small envelope in between his fingers. He said nothing for a few minutes, his handsome face very serious and unmoving. His smoulder only intensified by his obvious anger at the situation.

"You want to know my opinion?" I asked. I checked my phone quickly, still nothing from Eric.

"Is it going to cost me anything?"

"Hey, you already paid me to go to a strip club for you. Now you're going to bitch?"

He chuckled. "That's valid. Go ahead."

"I think you should let this go."

"Ok...?"

"She's not what you think she is, clearly. I'm not sure you want to get involved with, well, someone like her because you'll never know if it's real or she's just bamboozling you."

His eyebrows rose. "Bamboozled?"

Rolling my eyes, I sighed deeply. Clearly, I needed to be blunt. "She's a succubus, dude. I wish I was kidding but I'm not."

He stared blankly at me for a few more minutes, than tore open the note. His eyes scanned the page, and then he tossed it towards me before standing up and beginning to pace.

I grabbed it from where it landed on the coffee table and debated telling him to stop acting like a spoiled child before I read it. Lorcan Fitzpatrick clearly was not used to things not going his way, and he did not look pleased. For a moment I regretted not waiting for Eric to come with me.

"Look, I told you from the get-go that you might not like the response you get. Acting like a pissed off child doesn't do you any favours." I folded the note and put it back in my pocket when he wasn't looking.

"I don't like being lied to."

I checked my phone again. Still no Eric. "Neither do I. No one does. The way I see it you can either play this one of two ways. You already stink of desperation for hiring me to find her. You can either show up at Ren with some grand romantic gesture or you can forget she ever existed. A notch on what I am sure is your overly dented bedpost."

He laughed. "Is that what you really think of me?"

"You're freakishly good looking and the heir to the wolf pack. I'd be stupid if I didn't." I smiled at him. "If I were you, I would be man whoring it up like no other. But that's beside the point."

"What if me and the boys went to Ren and trashed the place?"

Now I laughed. "It's a Kinkaid bar. You feel like starting a war over her?"

"She works for them?"

"Beyond being an employee at Ren, I doubt it." I stood up and gathered my things. "Either way, my job is done. Unless you need anything else?"

"Sit down, Camille." He directed from between clenched teeth. Part of me wanted to laugh at him outright. Foolish child didn't know who he was fucking with.

Do you even hear yourself? He could probably kill you

three times before you hit the ground. Sit the fuck down, dumbass.

Reluctantly I sat back down, but made my irritation clear by my facial expression.

"You got five more minutes, golden boy. And I'm billing you." I kept my voice level.

"Can you make me a charm or a potion or whatever to get rid of whatever she did to me?" He looked away from me when he spoke, clearly embarrassed. Angry, but embarrassed. Not the best combo.

"No. But my people could. You have met Millie and her daughter."

"That's not going to happen. Looks like we're going to have to go talk to Moira."

"Who's Moira?"

12.

I followed Lorcan to his little black sports car he'd parked in the lot across the street. He drove way too fast, and I felt unprotected in his tiny two-seater death trap. I would most definitely be taking a different route home. Hopefully Eric reappeared soon.

"Where are we going?" I asked him.

"No one told you about Natural Causes?" He thankfully kept his eyes focused on the road as he spoke. "I keep forgetting this is new to you. I don't know exactly what Moira is, but she does magic. She might be a druid, high priestess or something. I don't speak that level of magic."

"And she's just cool with you walking in there with me?"

He shrugged. "I guess we'll find out."

Natural Causes turned out to be a health food store in The Annex neighbourhood, about a fifteen-minute ride in the death car from the clubhouse. I slung my laptop bag over my shoulder so I would be hands free, my purse pulled up high on the opposite shoulder. My gloves were on tight, and I felt as ready as I ever would be walking into unknown territory with a wolf I didn't trust.

Lorcan strode in like he owned the place, his general holier than thou attitude starting to piss me off. He went straight to the cashier, a younger girl with a long braid that hung down her back. She took one look at him, glancing briefly at me, and motioned for us to follow her.

Hope he is worth whatever happens next.

I grabbed my phone and began texting Eric my location as we navigated through a dark hallway into a large open back room.

Herbs hung from the ceiling in various bundles, and shelves lined the walls with different magical artifacts. Once I put my phone away, I found my eyes drifting around the room as I tried to take everything in.

I gravitated to a Polaroid photo that hung on the wall of three teenagers, two girls and one boy. The boy clutched an athame that sat on the shelf below it.

Is that the mom from the bus?

"Don't you think you should introduce yourself *blanchmains* before you start nosing around?" A female voice with a slight Irish accent made me jump. I turned to see an old woman sitting in a chair close to the center of the room, next to a cauldron. Her pale blue eyes watched me with curiosity, one half of her mouth turned up in a smile. She poked her opposite cheek and laughed as nothing moved on the other side of her face.

"Paralyzed. Doesn't work at all. Eye still does, but that's it." She laughed. "I'm Moira."

"Camille Bishop." I stuck out my hand to shake hers, she cackled when she saw my gloves.

"You Marie Le Fay's girl by any chance?" she asked.

"You knew my mother?"

"I did. But that's not why you're here." She looked up at Lorcan, swatting at him. "Got another one with pup, have you?"

I laughed loudly. "Oh, fuck no! Absolutely not! He's been bamboozled by a succubus."

"Have you now? It's a good thing you're pretty, boy." She leaned over and whispered to me. "He's very nice but a little light between the ears."

My eyes filled with tears as I began laughing probably a little too hard.

Lorcan raised his hand and said, "Is there something you can do about it? Something you can give me?"

"Cosima!" Moira called out to the younger girl. "Get the boy a talisman. And bring me a restoration vial."

Moira turned back to me. "That family of yours started teaching you anything?"

"A little. My mother bound my powers as a child, so I didn't find out until her immediate family killed my former boyfriend to unleash them." They all turned to me wide eyed when I finished. "In my defense, she told me her siblings and parents weren't around."

Moira sighed. "I told her it was a bad idea. We could

have guided you, eased you into it. It's a shame she died how she did. I'm sorry for that. I hope you know she was a good woman, just wanted to protect you."

I smiled, sadness pooling in the pit of my stomach. "I know. Thank you for saying that."

Cosima reappeared, and she helped Moira up so she could stand by the cauldron.

Their process of gathering ingredients and mixing in the cauldron looked different than Millie and Nya. Cosima chanted in a low voice through the entire process, and Moira spoke occasionally but I couldn't hear anything she said. Within about ten minutes a green glowing liquid filled the cauldron, steam rising up and into the room. It smelt of cedar and sweet grass.

Moira filled the vial and handed it to him, then dipped the talisman in the liquid and passed it to him as well. Lorcan put the leather cord around his neck and tucked it under his shirt, so it touched his skin.

"Take two drops of that until the bottle is empty." Moira gestured at him. "And stay the fuck away from it. You hear me? Leave this thing be!"

It took me a moment to clue in that when she said *it*, she meant Meg. From the look on his face, I felt pretty confident that he would listen.

He handed her some folded up money, I couldn't tell exactly how much. He said thank you and smiled at the two women.

"It was nice to meet you, Camille. Please come back again." Moira said, and I echoed the sentiment as I followed

Lorcan back out.

Once we got outside, I checked my phone. Eric finally reappeared and would collect me from here.

I tried to hide my disgruntled expression as Lorcan asked. "Can I drop you somewhere?"

"No, my ride will be here soon. And I wouldn't get back in that rolling death trap with you anyhow. Who taught you how to drive?" He tried to smile as I spoke, clearly thinking I was kidding. "I'm dead serious dude. That was scary."

He shrugged me off. "If I didn't say this earlier, thank you. I appreciate you doing this."

"I did the job you paid me for. I'm sorry it didn't turn out how you wanted it to."

"Nothing ever does." He turned away, got in his car and drove off without looking back.

Luckily within about ten minutes Eric pulled up. His car smelt quite fragrantly like bacon.

"You know the rental company might get mad that their car reeks like bacon, right?" I said once I got in and we started moving.

He shrugged. "Better than new car smell."

His jovial expression and casual tone made me think he didn't even realize that leaving the office and disappearing like that might make me feel bad. I debated internally whether it was worth the fight and ruining this new stage we got to in our relationship.

"So why did Lorcan bring you here?" Eric finally asked.

"He read Meg's note, got super pissy, and I told him what she is. He said something about taking his boys and trashing Ren, which I told him was fucking stupid as hell, then we came here. Moira gave him a talisman and a vial of restoration with some glowing green shit in it." I explained. "She's cool. I'd like to go back and talk to her one day."

"You told her who you are?"

"She knew when we walked in."

"Did Lorcan tell her?"

"No. I think she's just that powerful. Lorcan acted like a spoiled little baby. He needs a swift kick in the ass."

Eric shrugged. "He's essentially a prince. He was born into his position, unlike Liam who fought for it. That does things to your personality."

"I wonder what I would have been like if my mom hadn't bound my powers."

He turned to me as we stopped at a red light, and I saw something flash behind his eyes. A dark pulse, like a beacon shining out from his black pupils, crawled behind there waiting.

"Where did you go earlier?" I finally asked.

"When?"

"I went looking for you after another encounter with Lemme. Ted knew one of the women from the auction this morning, said she's a police detective."

"I was hungry, and I went out to get us some food. Yours is in a bag in the back."

"Oh. How come you didn't tell me?"

"I thought I would be back before you noticed I was gone."

"Where did you go?"

"I went back to the Burger King we stopped at by Ren."

"That's almost on the other side of town. Why would you go all the way over there? I'm sure there are closer ones if you Google it."

"I'm sorry, I didn't think me picking you up some lunch would be such an issue."

I put my hand on his shoulder. "It's not. And I appreciate it. Forget I said anything, ok? Where are we going now?"

"Do you want to go see if you can find Ledo, so you don't have to repeat the info about the lady in the photo?" He asked.

We stopped at a stoplight, and I nudged him, "Pull over for a sec."

Once we crossed the lights he pulled over at the side of the road and put the car in park. I leaned across the center console and grabbed his hands, pulling him towards me and kissing him. He seemed surprised as I cradled the back of his head with my hands, his hairs running through my fingers.

"I'm sorry, I was just confused. It was weird that you were gone, and I didn't know what happened." I said.

He smiled that same warm smile that made my heart melt. It would take time for me to pull back the crazy thoughts, and I couldn't use my shitty past experiences as an excuse forever.

"You don't need to worry about me like that, Cas." He kissed me softly on the cheek, turned the car back on and kept driving.

I ate my cold food in the car while Eric dropped off papers and did some other errands related to our job. I texted Ted and told him I wrapped up the Fitzpatrick file and that I would send Ramona the paperwork, also letting him know Eric and I were out and about and would not be back. I took his silence as a good thing.

The sun started going down as we pulled up at Millie's. I felt uncomfortable and stiff from sitting in the car for so long.

"You have any of my pain pills handy?" I asked before we got out of the vehicle.

He rolled his eyes. "You really need them?"

"I have been sitting in a vehicle for over an hour. Yeah, I need one. Two would be awesome."

"Maybe we should let Millie do another heal."

I chuckled. "Because it did so well the last time?"

He put his hand on the back of my neck and the warmth started to spread, then abruptly stopped.

"What the hell?" he looked down at his own hand, confused.

"Maybe we need to worry more about what's going on with you." I took his hand and kissed it softly. He leaned closer and kissed me again.

"We could come back later." I said quietly. "Go somewhere quiet and make out in your back seat for a while."

"If you think your neck hurts now." He touched my neck affectionately, rubbing his smooth and warm fingers along my skin.

I groaned. "Let's get this over with so we can go home."

"Yours or mine?"

"Yours, if that's cool. We can't be loud at mine." Before I got more sucked into kissing him, I turned and got out of the vehicle.

Millie looked happy to see us again when she answered, only this time she appeared wine free. Ledo and Nya were in the TV room at the back of the house which she guided us to.

"Anything cool happen with your compact?" I asked Ledo, cringing as I sat in the middle of the couch. Eric sat at my one side; Millie eyed me curiously as she sat at the other.

"Are you still in pain?" She asked.

"You bet. Healing potion not working. Met Moira today. Maybe she can help."

Millie looked offended. "How the hell did you meet Moira?"

"Lorcan Fitzpatrick. Long story." I took out my phone and brought up the photo Ted ID'd and handed it to Ledo. "Does the name Shae Rielle mean anything to you?"

"No. Why?" He handed me back my phone and I passed it to Eric.

"The blonde in that photo is Detective Shae Rielle. Her name is on a deed to a shop in Parkdale. Apparently, she has worked for the police for a while. My uncle Ted ID'd her immediately."

"Really? Do you know what the shop is called?" Ledo asked.

"Not off the top of my head. Give me a minute and I can look it up." I turned to pick up my laptop bag off my feet and pain began to throb in my neck and shoulder.

Eric dug around in his pocket and pulled out the prescription bottle, shaking one loose and handing it to me. I dry swallowed it without a word from anyone.

I leaned back on the couch and closed my eyes for a moment. "Give me a few minutes, will you?"

Ledo shrugged and got on his phone, I assumed using his own skills to look for anything about Shae Rielle.

"Are you alright?" Eric asked.

"Maybe riding in that tiny death trap with Lorcan made it worse." I confessed. At the time I didn't feel anything but now I didn't want to move at all if I could avoid it.

Suddenly my eyes glazed over, and that weird milkiness and feeling like a rubber band snapping forced me to blink hard a few times, then Lilly Darling stood behind Ledo's chair.

"What do you want?" I grumbled at her, closing my eyes again.

"You summoned me, chica. What's your problem?"

"Give me the low down on Moira."

She whooped out a laugh. "She did this to you? Then your fucking screwed, white hands."

"No. I met her today. This," I motioned over myself, "is something else."

"Moira is old magic. Like ancient. She used to work for

one of the demon hunting Orders before they got fucked and were destroyed. Now she's on her own. Pissing her off is a *bad* idea. Just ask Millie, she knows from experience." Lilly chuckled to herself. "For real, why did you summon me?"

"I didn't. I took a damn Percocet, leaned back and poof!"

"Who are you talking to?" Eric quietly asked.

"Lilly Darling." I whispered loudly.

"Can we get back on topic please?" Ledo asked. "Shae Rielle."

"Right!" I motioned to Eric. "Can you hand me my laptop please?"

"What the hell is wrong with you?" Lilly asked. "I know I called you a wet noodle before, but this is taking it a bit too far."

"While I have you here, what do you know about the mermaid in the tank at Nikki's lab?" I asked Lilly, opening an eye and watching her reaction. I'd brought it up before and she'd been cagey.

"Lord, are you still talking about that shit? Just let it alone already." Lilly exclaimed.

"Unless you have any useful information for me, please go away." I turned away from her and took my laptop, within a minute she disappeared.

Bringing up the deed for a place called Thesauri, I passed my laptop to Ledo. The pain in my neck still pulsed; I should have taken two pills.

"I wonder if she is the mystery woman from my dad's files." I mumbled to Eric, he squeezed my hand as my eyelids began to flutter and close.

"What's she talking about?" Ledo asked.

"There is a mystery woman buying relics for Kinkaid who may have stolen Excalibur." I kept my eyes closed as I spoke.

"Huh. Well, we should go to this place and check it out." Ledo sounded eager and excited.

I chuckled. "*We?* Like the private investigators should? Or are you included?"

Eric gently pat me on the arm. "We should get you home."

"Of course I'm included in the *we*. You wouldn't even know about the place if it wasn't for me." Ledo's tone felt sharp. Millie attempted to silence him but clearly he didn't get the hint. "No, Mom. She doesn't get to act that way just because...."

My eyes shot open, and my power reached across the room in his direction, snaking itself up his leg and beginning to coil around him.

"What the fuck?" Ledo asked. "Are you kidding me right now?"

"Stop it, Camille." Millie said angrily. I let it keep going; far enough that I could see in his eyes that it worried him. I turned my eyes to her, and she grabbed my wrist.

"You don't get to act that way in my house." Millie squeezed tightly, the pain diverting my thoughts away from my anger. "Until you get your shit under control, you need to leave."

I put my laptop in my bag and stood to leave. When Eric

didn't follow, I grabbed my shit and walked out.

13.

Storming off down the street in the dark, I got out my phone and tried to find the bus routes home. I figured at some point that Eric would come after me, but when I reached the main road and the bus stop appeared he still hadn't come. So, I fished my bus pass out of my purse and stood at the stop and waited.

Within about ten minutes it came, and I was on route home. He didn't call, none of them did. While I sat, I made a plan to check out Thesauri on my own tomorrow, mapping out bus routes and getting as much info about the place as I could. It appeared to be an antique store and curiosity shop.

I arrived home to a dark empty house. With no one home and no one calling, I decided to go through my father's files and gather a list of things to look for at Thesauri to try to connect them all.

The next morning, I woke up bright eyed and bushy

tailed, but my neck felt terribly sore. Tempted to text Eric and tell him to leave the painkillers in my office, I put the phone away from me. My focus needed to be on task today.

Ted stood at the stove making breakfast when I came down, Cuddy laughed at something on his phone. The scene warmed my heart, it felt like eons since our lives were normal like this.

Ted passed me a plate of eggs and bacon. "Morning sunshine. No lover boy today?"

"No. And shhh about him." I waved him off and sat down. "No Maritza today?"

Cuddy smiled to himself. "She's great. We're great. Life's great."

I laughed, his dopey lop-sided grin reminding me of when we were kids.

"How you feeling?" Ted asked. He sat down beside me, his cologne fresh and lemony. His warmth seemed to spread through the room, and I really felt at home.

"Sore but I'll live. Got a full day planned. Once I'm done work, I have a lead on something I found in my dad's files." I took a bite of bacon as Ted fully stopped.

"What sort of lead?" Ted's tone remained level.

"Oh! No, nothing with the Kinkaid stuff. I don't know if you remember them at all but there was information about some relics. I pieced some things together and I am going to an antique shop to ask some questions."

"Is Eric going too?"

"What? You don't think I can do it myself?"

"What's going on with you?" Both men turned and

stared me down.

"I don't know. Since the accident I have been off. I'm sorry." I looked back down at my food, their gaze too much for me to bear.

Ted reached over and put his hand on top of mine. "Just be careful, ok?"

"Of course." I kissed him on the cheek then went back to eating my food.

We chatted more about normal things going on in the world as we took Cuddy to school and drove to work. It felt great to be back to the way things were before everything changed, even if it turned out only to be brief.

When we got to the office Ramona grinned widely at me, enough that I paused at her desk.

"Good morning…?" I smiled back at her. "What did I do?"

"Nothing, sweetheart. But your boyfriend is in your office." I paused when she said the 'b' word, turning quickly to Ted who took off down the hallway.

"Thanks Ramona!" I tried to fake excitement, hopefully she didn't see through it.

I stopped just outside my door and listened. No noise, I couldn't even hear him breathing. Part of me wanted to rush in and apologise, the other wanted to walk by and go sit in his office and wait and see how long it took him to clue in. After thinking for a bit, I took a deep breath and stepped inside my office.

Hanging up my stuff and closing the door behind me, I

said nothing as I walked towards my desk. Sitting down so I could slide across, Eric put his hand on my knee.

"What happened yesterday?" his voice was low, non confrontational.

"I don't like his attitude. I don't like any of their attitudes, actually." I stayed where I was, watching his hand and wishing it would move higher.

"You know Millie is really hurt."

I chuckled. "So? I didn't hurt him. He was being a dick."

He grabbed my hand and pulled me down, so I straddled his lap. "You should have texted me."

I winced as I sat, my hand immediately going to my neck. "You could have texted me too you know."

"Are you ok?" he asked as he nuzzled my neck. I leaned into him, closing my eyes for a moment.

"Five by five. And you?"

He chuckled. "I missed you last night."

"Did they bitch about me after I left?"

"Ledo started to. But I left before he could say anything that would piss me off." He kissed the soft skin just below my ear. "Millie is just worried."

"That's kind of what Millie does."

"She has a point. That demon just disappeared without issue? That doesn't make sense from our experiences. I get why she would be suspicious."

The demon is gone because I gave it a body. But you don't need to know that.

"Why is it so hard to believe that I told it to fuck off and it listened? As you all have stated *repeatedly* you have never dealt with shit like mine before. Maybe you all should accept you don't know what you're talking about." I leaned down, kissing the side of his neck while moving my hands between his legs.

He laughed, a deep belly sound that made his body shake, and pulled my hands back. "Later, love."

"Why not now?"

"Because we're at work."

"What about the car?"

"You're in enough pain. I promise when our day is done, we'll go to my place and turn our phones off." He smelt my hair, and then used both hands to gently move me away.

I sighed loudly, sticking out my bottom lip in mock pout. "OK. Are you down to go to this shop with me and get a read on Shae Rielle? Maybe she knows where Excalibur is."

"Are we bringing Ledo?"

"Fuck no." He went to say something but before he could I kissed him. It didn't feel like an epic kiss, but it carried significance. Whatever happened last night could count as our first real fight.

"Hi." I smiled down at him, rubbing the pad of my thumb along his jaw.

He smiled back up at me. "Hi. I'm going to go make us some coffee. Then you can fill me in, and we can head out. What do we tell Ted?"

"I told him this morning. I'd planned the route if you and I didn't make up."

He laughed. "We can properly make up later." This time

he kissed me hard, the movement and his hand behind my head sent shivers down my spine.

Before it turned into *something* we separated, he went to make us coffee and I started on my official report on the Fitzpatrick file. Because Lorcan went to the trouble of making it official I needed to follow protocol and file a report.

Trying to find something to say that didn't make Lorcan come across as a total loser wasn't easy. He wouldn't get a copy of my official report unless he asked for it, and I couldn't imagine I would be hearing from him again in that capacity. So, I tried to be as honest as possible.

For normal eyes the situation looked like a black and white case of unrequited love. Cut and dry. Normally we wouldn't take those cases, too many dangerous variables. But I expressed quite clearly that the 'young Mr. Fitzpatrick' would not be an issue. And he wouldn't be.

While printing the report I also printed out my maps and a list for our little excursion today. I anticipated magic being involved, as it seemed to be in everything these days.

Are you a #Believer?

Two coffees' in and I felt ready to go. While Eric went back to his office to gather his things, I went to the reception area.

Ramona smiled as I came over. "Hello dear."

"Hey, do Eric and I have any appointments for the rest of the day?" I stood beside her desk and leaned down so I could see the calendar on her desktop.

"Client wise, no. You both have paperwork that needs to be filled out, but you don't have to be in the office to do that." Ramona shrugged, her curls bouncing. "Ted assumed you'd be on light duties for a while, and to be honest it's not like we have a lineup out the door."

"I wish they had bounty hunters in Canada."

"I know you do honey. You should really start going to the gym or something, take out that aggression on something more positive."

Eric appeared, travel mugs in hand. "You packed up?"

I smiled and nodded, waving by to Ramona as we returned to my office. Within minutes we were out the door, both laptops and my printed-out plans included. Feeling pretty confident, I laid out my ideas to Eric as we drove.

Turning my body towards him, I watched his every movement. Everything about me wanted to touch him; my magic, myself, my very being wanted to feel every part of him.

"You know they're probably not human, right?" Eric said.

I smiled, watching his lips move. "Huh?"

"Shae Rielle and this other woman, they're probably not human."

"So?"

"What if they are not too keen on the Merlin and *blanchmains* coming into their shop?"

"Then they shouldn't have opened a shop. This city is not that big, and we could always walk in randomly."

He chuckled. "Do you really believe that? You don't get how any of this works, do you?

"Nope. And I will use that to my advantage if need be."

"Playing dumb won't last forever." He began parallel parking the car, the shop not in clear view.

"Are we here?" I asked.

"I'm not going to park out front, silly. This isn't the best neighborhood so it's also about finding a safe place to park."

"I thought this was an up-and-coming area?"

"Up and coming doesn't necessarily take away the bad parts. As you'll see when we get out of the car. Make sure your door is locked and we'll lock the laptops in the trunk." He turned off the car, grabbed both our computer bags and went and locked them in the trunk. Turning to open the door, stiffness and soreness made it difficult to move. Taking a big breath in and out I pushed passed the pain and got out of the vehicle.

"You ok?" Eric held his hand out to me to help me up.

"Sore as hell. As soon as we're done, I will have to take some pain meds or something. I haven't had any since I left last night, and I am starting to feel it."

He put his hand right on the sore spot, pulling me close. The initial warmth felt soothing and eased the soreness a bit. I smiled, rolling my shoulders and moving into his embrace.

"You ready?" He asked quietly. Stepping away from him, I did a quick spin and took in our surroundings. The city's attempts to gentrify this once humble neighbourhood were obvious with the newly redone storefronts, but they were next to boarded up windows and doorways with sleeping homeless people. Once I got my bearings, I knew which direction we needed to go in.

Linking arms, we began walking on Queen Street West, one of the busier streets in Toronto. Eric seemed distant, gazing around at our surroundings like he'd never seen any of it before.

"Are you ok?" I asked him. "You seem a bit spaced."

He smiled down at me, a gleam in his eyes. "I'm good."

The black and gold sign came into view, dangling from a rot iron post about twenty feet above us with 'Thesauri' written in elegant script. The symbol I couldn't recognize from that far up but something about it made me keep staring.

"I think it's some kind of a protection rune." Eric traced a symbol in the air, leaving a pink glowing trail for a split second. "Old magic, but powerful."

"Older than ours?" I asked.

He paused, eyeing the symbol without looking at me. "Oh yeah."

Shit. Fuck.

"Well, let's go."

14.

Thesauri screamed elegant antiques. From the matte black paint around the outside, the gorgeous window display, to that same black with dark cherry wood throughout the interior with various displays everything looked classy. On the back wall in various mounts were swords of different shapes and sizes. A bell chimed overhead when we walked inside, it appeared very old when I glanced at it, with that greenish patina of aged bronze.

Something in the store made the palm of my hand tingle, like it vibrated somewhere inside, and I could feel it without touching it. My magic began to pulse up the same arm.

Whatever it is, it's calling me.

The copper haired woman appeared from a door at the back far left corner of the store, the frame covered in a black shiny curtain. She smiled brightly, brushing her long hair back behind her shoulder as she glided towards us.

"Hello! Welcome to Thesauri. Is there anything I can help you with?" With a slightly deeper voice for a woman, she radiated an energy that I never felt before.

I smiled brightly. "Hey there! We are just browsing at the moment."

"Please let me know if you require any assistance." Her smile never faltered, but I could see a glimmer that she noticed something about us. Grabbing Eric's hand, he gave me a strange look when our skin touched.

"Something likes me I think." I whispered. "I feel a weird vibration."

"This is where Ledo may have been useful." He reminded me and I jabbed him in the ribs. "What? It's true."

We started looking through the different displays, finding various objects ranging from jewellery to other random knickknacks. The tingling in my hand started to get worse, turning into more of a prickly feeling, causing me to constantly clench and unclench my hand.

Nothing in particular stuck out to me in the shop. My sleeves were pulled down over my hands even though I wore my gloves. But something, *something* in that store called out to my magic in a way that I didn't fully understand.

Could it be her?

She carried herself differently than most women. She stood tall and proud in a way that I'd not seen before. No wonder Ledo drooled.

When I looked at her, I could see her in gold armour with a spear and a shield.

"Cas, you gotta stop staring." Eric's voice brought me out of my thoughts. Blinking quickly, my eyes began to water as I turned my head. A tear dripped down my cheek.

A rustle of noise from across the room and Shae Rielle came out from behind the curtain. A purple glow framed her body; it reminded me of the mom on the bus the other day.

Wasn't she in a Polaroid at Moira's?

"Cas you're really staring." Eric whispered harshly, and the two women turned around. They watched us curiously, like a cat watching a mouse deciding if it's worth the effort or not.

The copper haired woman came back over to us, holding out her hand and saying, "My name is Otrera. This is my shop."

Putting out my gloved hand, she smiled slightly before taking it, and an electric shock shot up through my arm and made me jump back. Eric must have felt it too because he jerked back from me in a sudden movement.

Otrera kept a firm grip on my hand. "Well, young lady. Do you want to tell me exactly who both of you are, and what you are doing in my store?"

15.

We stood silent for a few minutes, unsure of how to react. Something about the way her dark grey eyes bared down on me; I knew I needed to be honest for us to walk out of here intact.

"We saw you both at the auction a few days ago and thought you might be able to help us with a lead." My smile grew bigger as I spoke, trying to appear friendly. "We didn't know what you, or that you…."

Now she laughed. "And what exactly do you think I am, little girl?"

"Not sure. But your friend has a pretty purple glow." I nodded to Shae Rielle, who laughed loudly.

"You know my name, but you have yet to tell me yours." Otrera kept my hand in a firm grip, I wondered if she noticed the tingling.

"Camille Bishop."

Shae smiled brightly. "Bishop? Any relation to former Detective Ted Bishop and…."

"Ted is my uncle, and my boss."

"Which makes you a P.I.?"

"Yes, but that's not why I am here."

Shae got up and moved closer. "And what about Will Bishop?"

I turned my eyes to her now and smiled. "My father."

Shae poked Otrera in the side. "Let her go. This is Marie's girl."

"You knew my mother?" My voice croaked out.

"We did. I'm sorry for what happened to both your parents." Otrera let go of my hand. "You're here about your father's files, I presume?"

The room stopped, waiting for me to respond. With the millions of questions swirling through my mind, I decided that continuing to be honest made the most sense.

"I am, actually. But what does that have to do with my mother?"

"Come, let's have some tea and discuss." They motioned us towards the black curtain; I followed and dragged Eric along behind me.

The back room looked more like a living room, clearly where they entertained higher level clientele. Everything looked expensive. I felt guilty sitting on the plush green velvet couch they directed us to.

"You look like her." Otrera said as she poured the tea.

I looked quickly at them both. "Pardon?"

"Your mother." Otrera smiled warmly when she finally sat across from us. "I'm surprised I didn't recognize you earlier. If you cut your hair shorter, I would have thought you were Marie."

"Thank you." Tears clouded my vision. "I am guessing if you knew her you knew who she was."

Shae laughed. "You le Fay are hard to miss. Marie went to great lengths to conceal what she was from Will. To hide our world in general actually. He found us because on occasion we procure items for Gabriel Kinkaid."

That name was new. "I don't know that person."

"You've never heard of Elliot Kinkaid's brother? Actually, that doesn't surprise me. He's not one to be out in public." Shae took a sip of her tea.

"Well, regardless of all her hard work, Gabriel found out about Will. Neither of the Kinkaid's would ever stoop that low to get their hands dirty, but they sent their goon squad." Shae looked away from me. "I was part of the team at the scene. I'm so sorry."

White hot rage bubbled through me. "Was there any evidence?"

"Not directly. But, like you, I have this…. sense when it comes to death." Shae smiled. "I knew it was them but could never openly prove it. Are you here because you're seeking revenge?"

About to say something, I stopped midway. Then I really let what she said process, and I felt unsure what to say.

"I'd never really thought about revenge, to be honest. I want justice. I was raised to believe in justice." I took a sip of my tea. "I wanted to ask you some questions about Excalibur and about that flame sword from the auction."

"Those young women, I believe were from the Cult of Guinevere." She laughed when she noticed my shocked expression. "You never heard of them? They are practically built into your mythology."

I looked to Eric. "Ring any bells to you?"

"And who are you, exactly?" Otrera asked.

"My name is Eric. I'm the Merlin." Their eyes widened a bit when he spoke.

"Really?" Otrera grinned. "We have some items belonging to some of your predecessors, if you're ever interested in looking."

"So, why are you here then?" Shae asked. Both of their eyes turned to us, and I felt a wave of something wash over me. Their magic swelled and filled the room, a clear sign not to try anything stupid. It prickled down my arm and my hand still hummed with energy.

"Truthfully?" I met both their gazes, taking my gloves off as I did. My plaster pale hands reached out and picked up my tea and took a sip. "I'm looking for Excalibur."

Otrera and Shae exchanged glances and smiled at each other. Eric tensed beside me.

"Since we walked in the building my hand has been tingling." Opening my right palm, I held it out to examine it.

"Your sword hand is singing." Otrera chuckled.

"What are you two exactly?"

"Something very old. But that is a story for another day. Have you got money?"

"What do you mean?"

They both laughed. "We're a business my dear. I can't

just hand it to you for free."

I thought long and hard about any money I'd saved. My nest egg I collected for Jesse and I grew quite a lot. The plan for the money originally consisted of me buying a condo and him moving in with me. It wasn't much of a plan, but it gave me hope for the future.

There should be a down payment in that account now, which would hopefully pay the deposit on Excalibur if they had it.

"Do you have it?" Eric asked, and the room fell silent. To me it seemed obvious, but no one else could feel the strange pulsing in my hand.

Your sword hand is singing.

If I remembered the stories correctly, the sword *belonged* to Arthur. The Lady of The Lake gave it to him; I knew nothing of the sword before the Lady handed it to Arthur.

"Before you get into that explain this Cult of Guinevere." I said.

"Their mission is to tell Guinevere's *true* story. They believe that her tale was lost in fiction, or something like that. Also she was just as much of a warrior as Arthur, and he married her because she was an equal. Yes, it was a love match, but she was a great queen in her own right. Apparently." Otrera said.

"What about the affair?"

Otrera laughed. "An attempt to besmirch her good name. In some circles they believe Lancelot is a woman."

"You'll have to tell me where you learned all this from

so I can check it out myself." My head swam with so many questions.

"Well, once we found what we believed to be Excalibur we had to prove it. Nothing works in my industry unless you can validate it. I suppose that's similar to yours, isn't it?"

"And do you do this for higher brow people than the Kinkaid's?" I asked.

"Absolutely. They're positively low brow compared to our normal clientele."

"Did they introduce you to Dr. Frankenstein?"

That made them both pause. "Who?"

"Dr. Frankenstein and his however many times granddaughter are in their employ, or however you say it. Sorry speaking proper is not my forte. They also apparently have a mermaid in a tank in their lab."

Shae immediately tensed, putting her hand on Otrera's shoulder. "A mermaid? How can you be sure?"

"I have it on good authority from a very credible witness. She has been trying to get me to go rescue her, which we have no hope of pulling off on our own."

"But we could." Shae's eyes grew glassy. She and Otrera locked eyes and I saw something, a spark between them so beautiful and pure that I felt privileged to witness it. I sat in the presence of a once in a lifetime connection. A bond like no other. I wondered if they rode into battle together. The story of the mermaid also got much more interesting.

"So, you never answered my question. Do you have Excalibur?"

Silence fell over the room. We all stared at each other,

waiting for anyone to move and react. The mere mention of my sword sent tingles through my hand and up my arm. Maybe they thought I would just go for it, but even I didn't have that big of a death wish. While they may appreciate my boldness to a certain extent, I couldn't imagine this would be a good time to demonstrate.

Otrera smiled. "What do you think? Your sword hand is singing."

"I don't know what to think. This is all really new."

Shae held out her open palm in front of me, slowly closed her hand into a fist and saying a few quiet words, then her fingers unfurled, and a sword appeared in her hand. Up the middle of her wrist and forearm a series of intricate tattoos flared gold then disappeared.

"Whoa." My voice was quiet and a little breathless.

"If we truly have Excalibur, and it is *your sword, blanchmains,*" Shae began, "than you should be able to summon it."

I closed my eyes and took a breath, concentrating on the vibration in my hand. The little tingles, the prickling, the sparks that seem to shoot up my arm. Holding my hand palm up, my fingers outstretched, when I curled them up a strange burning sensation started on the inside of my wrist.

Uncurling my fingers, I could feel sparks coming to life, shooting bits of electricity as I continued to pull my them apart.

Suddenly there was something in my hand, a physical mass that materialized from nowhere. Closing my fingers again, cold hard metal vibrated against my skin.

I opened my eyes and, sure enough, I now held a sword. The sword.

My sword.

"Jesus." I blurted out. "Could I have done this the whole fucking time? Is this another thing on the list of bullshit being kept from me?"

Swinging the sword from left to right, only casually so I wouldn't hurt anyone; it felt right in my hand. I never thought I would ever in my life *want* a sword let alone to wield one.

As I moved my arm, I noticed an interlacing pattern in lines of black that wound up, with a large sword at its centre, its point directed towards my wrist and hilt to my elbow.

"That's new." I held my arm towards Eric who began to examine it. "Is it going to stay forever or come and go? It'll be a hard one to explain to Ted."

Shae laughed. "Your uncle is a good man. It's really too bad his partner is not."

Eric and I both turned to her. "Excuse me?"

Shae waved us both off as Otrera began to speak. "So, clearly the sword is yours."

"How much?" I asked.

She leaned closer to me. "How much you got?"

Reaching into my purse, I pulled out my wallet and rifled through what I had on me. Leaning over the table, she pulled a five-dollar bill from my wallet.

"Would you like a receipt?"

"I don't understand." I pointed the sword down, thinking

I wished I could put it somewhere, and when I wiggled my fingers, it vanished. The tattoo did not.

"I couldn't very well have it getting around that I didn't charge you, now could I? But I could not in good conscience make you pay for something you are already bonded with in such a way." She waved the bill in front of us. "Now you have paid. We're square."

"Where did it go?" I asked. Otrera got up and went back out into the store, returning with a leather scabbard and sheath, my sword clearly inside.

We both stood as she handed it to me. There were no words; I could barely form a coherent thought, so I prayed Eric did better. There was *no way* it would be this easy.

Nothing works out this good for you. Ever. There has to be some kind of catch. You'll walk 10 feet outside and get smoked by a toilet seat from an exploded plane or some shit. Or they want you to sign over your first born.

Looking at them both, the sword clutched firmly in my hand, I said, "This all seems too easy. There has to be a catch."

"I don't know if it's a catch. Call it a caveat. You can tell no one where you got that from." Otrera began. "And this lab where you say the mermaid is? We want any details you have. Plans, maps, descriptions, anything. Along with whatever you have on Dr. Frankenstein and his granddaughter."

"Can I ask why? I made a promise to a friend that I would rescue that mermaid." I sighed. "I'm not even sure I believe it's still there."

"Would your friend be alright if you told her the mermaid will be rescued, but you are not involved?"

"Can you guarantee that she will?"

"If she is still there, she will be."

Contemplating her statement, I wondered about their connection. These two were certainly old and powerful but I could get no read off exactly *what* they were. Sending in the cavalry to take on Frankenstein could prove to be a really bad idea.

Or a really fucking great one, dummy. They look like the really damn big stone you get to kill two birds with.

Maybe they would end up killing Bliss too.

Looking down at my new tattoo, the interlacing lines now gone and the sword more prominent, there wasn't much else I could say.

"Will you keep me updated?"

They both seemed surprised. "Absolutely."

"Then we have a deal."

16.

Leaving Thesauri, I felt like I accomplished a lot. With an ally that possessed some actual legit power, I gained new confidence.

Even if I never saw them again, it didn't matter. I had my sword.

Staring mindlessly at my new tattoo as we drove, I couldn't help but smile. Eric and I hadn't spoken since we walked out of the shop, my mind completely on the newest addition to this insanity.

The next time I looked back up we were back at the office. I turned to Eric.

"We're here?" I said. "I thought we were going to…."

"I have something I have to take care of." He didn't look at me as he spoke, something seemed off about him, but I couldn't put my finger on it. Gathering up my things, he made no move to embrace me as I got out of the vehicle and took my laptop out of the trunk. I did my best to drape my coat over the sword, hoping it wasn't visible. Before I could get to the driver's side door to say goodbye, he honked his horn and drove away.

Standing in the parking lot like an asshole, I watched him drive away until he went out of sight. That damaged part of me that clung to a shitty relationship screamed to call him, chase him down, probe until I got the response I wanted. But logically the rational part of me knew that wouldn't solve anything.

And he still has your pain meds.

Dragging myself back into the office, Ramona looked surprised to see me. Smiling and nodding felt difficult, but I managed a passable expression and got into my office without her following me. Putting all my stuff down I slithered over my desk and started rummaging through my drawers for some sort of pain medicine. I'd settle for Midol if necessary.

My hasty ransack came up short, so I went into the break room and began going through the cupboards.

"Whatcha looking for?" Ted's sing song voice made me jump.

"Jesus, you scared the shit out of me." I turned and smiled at him. "You don't have any pain killers on you, do you? Eric split and he's got my meds, and my neck is screaming in pain."

He shrugged. "Sorry kid, maybe ask Ramona. I thought you guys would be gone most of the day, I'm surprised to see you."

"We went and did some things, and he said he had to

take care of something and dropped me off."

"He didn't say what or where he was going?"

I shook my head. "Nope."

"That's weird for him?"

"A little."

"Did he mention Chris sending him out for something?"

The odd query about his partner made me pause. "Nope."

"Well, maybe text him in a bit. Cuddy has been talking about having Maritza over for dinner and I thought it would be nice if we all ate together."

Opening my mouth to speak, I quickly closed it. Perhaps they were right, and I needed to find a way to accept the fact that this Maritza character wasn't going anywhere. Immediately I thought of calling Millie but decided against it.

"Alright. We can do that. I got a random question for you. Have you ever heard of Gabriel Kinkaid?"

His head tilted to one side. "Elliot Kinkaid's brother. What about him?"

"I was just curious what you knew about him. What he does for a living, is he local, shit like that."

"Well, that's an easy one. There's nothing to know. He's been dead for, well, I want to say fifteen years? But maybe it's been longer. Why? Where did you hear that name from?"

I shrugged. "In my dad's files. I'd never heard the name before, so I was curious."

"Not much to tell really." His phone beeped, he quickly checked it then stood with his coffee in hand. "But we can talk about him on the ride home if you want."

"Sounds good." I followed him back towards Ramona's desk, he waved as he continued on back to his office.

Smiling big and showing off teeth, I leaned on the side of Ramona's desk. One of the most retro things in the office, a ledge for people to sign forms or other random things sat about a foot above the actual desktop. It reminded me of something from the 1960s.

"Hey, do you have any pain medicine by any chance?" I said sweetly. "Eric has my pills, and he went out and I am in quite a lot of pain."

She nodded quickly, opened the top drawer of her desk, withdrew one of several bottles of pills, shook two into her hand and handed them to me. "You'll have to wait a few hours to take any more, but I can send you home with a couple to tide you over until he brings your meds back."

I smiled warmly, closing my hand. "Thank you. I really appreciate it."

Quickly squeezing my hand, the phone started ringing so I took that as my chance to bail and started down the hall. I stopped at my door for a moment, considering something, and then continued to Eric's office.

The door sat slightly ajar, and I quietly peeked inside. No sign of him reappearing, and a quick glance around it looked like he hadn't been here at all, even though I knew he had. Going inside, I sat at his desk and began to rummage around. When I opened his top desk drawer, sure enough, I found a small earwax orange plastic bottle with a white lid that I quickly shoved in my pocket. Beside it sat a phone number written on the back of a business card, the ink terribly smudged to the point that I almost couldn't read it.

But I would recognize Bliss's number anywhere. Quickly flipping the card over, Ren's neon logo looked like a giant warning sign.

Why would the demon give that phone number to Eric?

Taking a photo of both sides of the card, I put it back where I found it. Maybe it was innocent; the demon spoke about him before. Maybe it thought it could be sneaky.

Or maybe Bliss was crying out from inside for help.

I left his office exactly as I found it, dry swallowing the pills Ramona gave me on my way back to my office. As soon as he saw that the pills were gone, he would know I looked around, but I didn't want him to think I'd been snooping.

Once my door closed, I considered tracking his phone. I couldn't keep doing this; I didn't want to be *that* person again. Having an adult relationship meant behaving like an adult; my inclining towards jealous teenage bullshit wasn't attractive. So, I decided my time would be better spent doing other things, first off keeping up my end of the bargain by sending Otrera and Shae that information.

It took some time for me to scan all the papers Lemme brought me. When I previously read them, the info hadn't really processed, but now at second glance I could see my friend's descent into madness plain as day. That made me sad. But this would be that mermaid's best chance of survival without starting a full out war.

So, what are you going to tell Lemme, genius? Hey, I

found two chicks that, well, I don't know what the fuck they are, but they are going to rescue the mermaid. And don't worry! It was part of the bargain that I got my sword with so I'm eighty five percent sure they will honor it.

It took longer than it should have for me to realize that Eric may have an issue with me having the sword. A pretty clear sign that the pills kicked in and I could avoid deep thinking for a while.

Easing back in my chair I got super lost in my thoughts until the phone rang.

"Hey kid." It seemed like forever since I'd heard Kiera's voice. "Staying out of trouble?"

I laughed. "Never! Why? What's up?"

"I have to tell you something really important. Are you busy?"

"Nope. What's up?"

"Are you sitting down? Maybe you should go get Ted."

"Oh balls. Who's dead now?"

"No! No one. But there has been a development in Jesse's case."

"A development? What do you mean?" I swallowed hard, biting back my anxiety.

"Well, we arrested this prostitute recently. She was more than just a prostitute, she was a stripper and a porn star...... wait, are you ok to hear this? I don't want to upset you."

The first line of that bitch's email burned into my thoughts. "I'm fine. Just tell me."

"OK so, we had been watching this girl for a while. We

got a tip that she had been drugging guys to get them to stay with her, a concerned mother called us worried about her son. So, we went to check it out, and caught her red handed over top of a body."

"What does this have to do with Jesse?"

"Well, we got a search warrant for her place and her phone. Not only did she have photos of Jesse on her phone, but she had his ID, and the silver promise ring you gave him in eighth grade."

I'd forgotten all about that stupid ring. "How do you know it was his?"

"Because your name is engraved on it, silly. Why would I say it was his if I didn't know for sure?"

Wow. Had the le Fay set that up or was it just a random coincidence?

"Holy Shit." All I could manage to say, my mind gone so fucking blank I almost forgot how to speak.

"*I know, right?* I know it's a lot to process, but this is a good thing. She will be brought to justice. And maybe it will bring you some peace."

"What do you mean?"

"I don't know, I thought it might help you knowing he didn't do this to himself."

I know that. He's dead because of me.

"Camille? Camille? Are you ok?"

Shaking my head, I said, "Yeah. I'll be alright. Keep me posted on the whole situation. Can you tell me her name?"

"It'll be on the news in the morning but as long as you don't go try to scoop the story." She chuckled at her preposterous statement. "Her name is Amanda. Amanda Foster."

I sighed. "Of course it is."

"You know this girl?" Kiera chuckled. "Of course you do."

"Remember the illegally obtained brothel video from before?" She groaned as I continued. "That's Amanda. Jesse was having an affair with her."

"Great. What do you know about her?"

"Not a lot. Stripper, whore." I thought about the last thing Jesse said about her, whether or not I should mention it. "Jesse told me some story about her drugging his food to keep him there, and he would start withdrawing when they were apart for too long and he'd go back. Sounded like bullshit to me."

"I gotta run, kid. We'll talk more later." Kiera hung up before I could continue.

Putting my phone down on my desk, racing thoughts made me stop. I leaned my elbows on the tabletop and held my head in my hands.

Considering everything that happened to me, you'd think that when fate pointed me in a direction that I wouldn't be surprised anymore. And this, this was a clear and obvious sign from somewhere that Jesse would have died anyway.

It still messed with my head, the knock at my door bringing me back to reality.

By the look on Ted's face, I knew that he talked to Kiera. Grabbing my stuff, I crawled out from behind my desk.

"Ready to go home?" He put his big warm hand on my

shoulder. I nodded slowly. With my eyes pointed down I followed him out to the car.

Closing my eyes as Ted drove, I leaned back and with my neck supported on the headrest, the vibration of the moving vehicle actually felt good.

"You ok?" Ted's voice was oddly quiet.

"You talked to Kiera?"

He hesitated. "Yeah."

"It's the girl from the brothel. The one from the video Q took. I think you got video of her too."

"Oh good."

I opened one eye and turned to him, "I'm not sure she did it."

"That's for the police to figure out. Did you hear from Eric at all?"

"Nope."

"You haven't mentioned Millie lately. Everything ok on that end?"

Nope. "Sure. But it's like I said before, she's my mom's people. Doesn't mean she's mine."

"I knew your mom pretty well, and for a long time. If Millie was your mom's people, I am sure she would have been mentioned it least once and I had never heard of her until you told me who she was."

Letting that statement process, I paused for a while before saying, "Valid point."

The car stopped moving, and I opened my eyes and we were home.

"Do you need help?" Ted asked as I opened my door.

"I'll scream if I do." He laughed as he got out ahead of me, standing by the hood of the car waiting as I slowly got out. He watched me with a big silly grin on his face, like I was learning to ride a bike or something.

"I was hurt, not broken." I told him as I linked arms with him, my laptop and purse slung over the same shoulder and my coat draped over the sword in my other hand.

The house seemed empty, with an odd stillness that made the hair on the back of my neck stand up.

"Does something feel off to you?" I asked Ted.

He stopped, stood silently for a moment, and then said, "No. Seems fine to me."

Nodding my acceptance, I took off my things and continued into the house. But that feeling, which now tingled up my arm, I couldn't shake.

The familiar click of a can opening, and I knew Ted settled in front of the TV and I could walk the house alone. Leaving my coat downstairs, I hid the sword behind my back as I quietly walked around.

A quick check and I found nothing. When I got back to my room and closed the door, just for the hell of it I summoned the sword.

It felt completely different to when I summoned a ghost, more powerful and far less scary.

But it burned. My new sword shaped tattoo burned like a brand, and I doubled over in pain. My fingers closed around the heavy metal hilt, and something inside me surged to life.

Smiling, I wiggled my fingers again and the sword

disappeared, back into the scabbard on my bed.

I sat down beside it, pulling out my phone to call Eric. It rang three times before he answered.

I heard a bunch of loud noises before he said, "Hello?"

"Hey." Staying quiet for a moment, I tried to identify some of what I heard. "We're at home now. I didn't want you to go back to the office if you didn't have to."

"But I have to go back to the office to get Cas." His voice sounded oddly flat.

"I am Cas, silly." I tried to chuckle. "Didn't my name pop up on your call display?"

"What? Cas? What are you talking about?"

I stayed quiet for a minute, listening to his background noise, "Where are you?"

"I'm driving. I can't talk when I'm driving. I'll call you when I am home." Click.

That was weird.

Stashing the sword under my bed, I went back downstairs to grab my laptop to track his phone.

17.

Quickly grabbing my laptop, I opened the software we'd used to track Jesse's phone. It felt like eons ago that Q, Lemme and I went on our little adventure, but it really wasn't. It amazed me that so much crazy could happen in a matter of weeks.

As I input the information my phone rang. Sighing, believing it to be Eric, I picked it up without checking the call display.

"Hey, what happened?" I said.

Millie chuckled. "I was hoping you would tell me."

Crap. I debated what to say, finally deciding on, "Oh. Hey."

"C'mon, Camille. You can do better than that."

"I don't know what you want me to say. That boy of yours was being a dick. I just wanted to scare him. That's all."

"That's all? Camille, you could have really hurt him."

I groaned loudly. "Don't be so dramatic. I would have stopped before he got seriously hurt."

"I don't want to argue with you. I called because I'm worried about Eric."

"Why? What did he do?"

"Is he with you?"

I hesitated. "Not at the moment."

"Well, where is he?"

"I am actually trying to figure that out as we speak."

She got quiet, and I heard a male voice in the background. She growled, and then said, "Ledo wants to know if you guys went to Thesauri."

"Not important right now. Why are you worried about Eric?"

"He's been off lately. Something doesn't seem right about him."

"Since when?"

"Since…. well, since the accident."

I laughed. "We've both been off since the accident, Millie."

"You, yes. But him, this is something else."

"Something else like what?"

"I know what you're going to say, but maybe the demon…."

"Urgh, my God! How many times to I have to tell you? The demon is GONE!"

"Well, I don't believe that, Camille."

"*Why the fuck not?*"

"Because it's *never* that simple!"

Moving the phone away from my face, I debated my next move. Hanging up on her seemed logical, but if something ended up being seriously wrong with Eric, I would need their help whether I wanted it or not. But in no way would I knuckle under. Not for a second.

"I don't know what to tell you. To the best of my knowledge, the demon is no longer an issue. I've not even seen a trace of it since that night we had the showdown with Nikki Frankenstein. Maybe she trapped it somehow."

Millie covered the mouthpiece of her phone and cussed at someone. I suspected that Ledo would not give up so easily.

"I told you he's being a dick." I rolled my eyes at myself, my voice sounded just like my cousin Poppy's.

"He's pretty adamant that you're hiding something. He's got this crazy idea in his head that you've got Excalibur now." She laughed awkwardly. "That's crazy, right? The sword has been missing for hundreds of years. You couldn't have just randomly stumbled on it."

I held my phone to my ear with my shoulder and began typing Eric's info into the tracking software on my laptop. "Nope, no sir. No randomly stumbling."

"What are you doing?"

I silently waited as the software calibrated his location, praying to whoever would listen that he wasn't where I suspected him to be. Wishing that, for once, things could be normal and calm and not get so stupidly fucked up.

The program beeped and a map popped up on my screen. I took a breath, leaned over, and looked at it.

"Goddammit!" I yelled. Waving my hand in the air, the contents of my desktop except my laptop went flying across the room.

"What?" Millie asked.

"He's at fucking Ren."

"What? Why the hell would he be at Ren?"

"I gotta go. I'll call you back if I need help." I tossed my phone on the bed, holding my head in my hands. That horrible sinking feeling that consumed so much of my life came back with a vengeance, and all I wanted to do was lie down and close my eyes. I figured with Jesse dead and buried I would never feel this feeling again.

Maybe he wasn't the problem all along.

Maybe it's me.

The bottle of pills felt heavy in my pocket, the invasive thought drilling a hole into my mind. *Take two more. You won't feel a thing.* If I did that all along, if I succumbed to the temptation that seemed to be always around me, my life would have gone down a very different path, regardless of the direction someone else tried to push it in.

Thinking briefly of my mom, I pushed her out of my thoughts. The last thing I needed to do was summon her unprepared. With so many questions that only she could answer, when would be the right time? Who else would have to die before I felt ready to face her?

Shaking my head, my fractured mind hoped the bad thoughts would just somehow fall out. Like they would scatter similar to how leaves fall off a tree during a windstorm. Now was a time I truly needed to be alone with my thoughts without any ghostly intruders.

Right now, I needed to dial back and think logically. There was no guarantee that he went to Ren to talk to the Bliss demon. We'd just seen Meg, maybe she bamboozled him.

And he went back to get sex eaten by a succubus? Ew.

That particular line of thinking could easily be solved by calling Meg. But if she bamboozled him, she would lie about it. Did I really want to threaten her over something that might not involve her at all? I could also call Bliss's phone and talk to the demon. Not that I think it would be honest.

Closing my eyes, I attempted to calm myself. As I took in a big breath, the computer beeped, and I opened my eyes to see that the little dot began to move on the map.

Even now, knowing that he could be in serious trouble, I felt like an asshole watching that little blip move. The only person, or people, that I trusted more than Eric were Ted and Cuddy. Deep in my very core, I knew that he would never do anything like the shit Jesse pulled. Not in a million years. It wasn't because I was so special and whatever, but Eric just wasn't *that* guy.

Watching closely, the blip seemed to speed through the city in the direction of Eric's house. Secretly I wished that he came here, but knowing now that he went somewhere safe, I felt a bit better. As soon as the blip stopped for longer than a few seconds my phone rang, and I believed he parked at his home.

"Hello?" I answered on the second ring, trying not to

sound too overly eager.

"Hey." Out of breath, he practically panted into the phone.

"You ok? Sounds like you've been running."

He continued to breathe heavily, and something inside me wanted to scream. A primal part of me, maybe the part of Nimue and Merlin that were linked so long ago, went into beast mode and I became so caught up with emotion I started to cry.

"Camille?" He began to speak normally, his confused tone becoming clear and direct. "Camille, what's the matter? Are you alright?"

"Are you?" I took a few cleansing breaths, attempting to calm myself. Some therapist long ago tried to teach me breathing exercises to help calm anxiety. That shit must be good for something.

"Absolutely. Why? What happened?"

"You dropped me off then you were gone, and I called you earlier..."

"Sorry. I had to go take care of something for Lewis that I forgot about. I'm such an idiot I passed out in my car during a stake out."

"Why didn't you tell me? I would have come with."

"I would not have expected you to sit in a vehicle with me for hours while you're in pain. That's a dick move." He stopped, listening to my shaky breaths and I calmed down. "Look, you're going to have to trust me, or this is never going to work. You can't freak out every time I'm not there."

My head lowered. "I know. It wasn't just that. Millie

called earlier saying she was worried about you."

"And it sent you on some shit spiral? You should know better than that, Camille."

"I know. I'm sorry. This is all new, and I'm trying."

"Ok. And I will try to be more forthcoming."

"Thank you. Oh hey, Ted said something about us all having dinner here one day with the Maritza girl."

"That sounds interesting."

"And fucking Ledo was bitching at Millie in the background when she called, he wanted to know if we went to Thesauri, and he thinks I'm hiding something."

"Did you tell her about the sword?"

"No."

"Then you're hiding something."

"I just got it. I don't want to report back to them like they run my life somehow."

"I know. But it would be good to keep them in the loop." He yawned. "I just walked in the door though. I'll call you back in a bit."

"OK. Bye." We hung up and I cried as I put my phone on the bed.

Stop, you dumbass. Why the hell are you crying? You're the one acting like a baby. How could you forget that Lewis is the reason your dumb ass went to Ren in the first place? Why would he not send his fucking protégé there? You're upgrading from limp noodle to bottle of mush.

Standing up, I jumped up and down and tried to shake off the shitty feelings. It'd been a while since I'd stayed home and hung out with Ted and Cuddy, so I would do exactly that.

A quick change into some sweats and an old t-shirt and I immediately felt comfortable. I headed downstairs to help Ted with dinner, hanging out in front of the TV with him when everything finished. It felt good to have a quiet night at home. Cuddy announced to us both that Maritza would be coming for dinner tomorrow, so I texted Eric that it was on like Donkey Kong.

The next morning, I woke up in a haze. Whatever Ramona gave me worked for pain but played hide and seek with the rest of my brain power. I prayed a hot shower, and some coffee would wash that away.

With a normal, regular business as usual morning, I felt good walking into the office. The two Percocet I took with breakfast of course helped with the smile on my face. Eric wasn't there when we arrived, so I decided to wait in his office with coffee as he often did in mine.

As I walked down the hallway towards his office, I noticed Chris Lewis's door sat open and he seemed to be getting organized for the day. He walked past the door, dressed to the nines in a perfectly tailored navy-blue suit. He turned when he saw me, smiling and nodding as I walked by. I did the same, as he went out of sight Shae Rielle's words bounced around in my mind. I'd always known Chris Lewis wasn't perfect, no one pretended he was. But I never would have believed at his core he wasn't *a good man*. It seemed very strange to me that Ted would align himself with someone who wasn't good, but maybe

I was being naïve.

Maybe Ted had no clue who Chris Lewis really was.

With the chair angled so the door didn't hit me, I put the coffee cups down on his desk and waited. After a few minutes I took out my phone and began mindlessly scrolling to pass the time. I knew he would be here soon.

But time ticked on, and he didn't appear. Drinking my coffee slowly, when I finally heard his footfalls in the hallway it felt almost cold.

I smiled brightly when Eric appeared, trying my best to hide my annoyance. "Good morning sunshine!"

He smiled when he saw me; a different kind of warmth came to it when he saw there was coffee. Shutting the door behind him, he dropped his stuff into a heap on the ground.

"It's probably cold by now." I said as he went straight for the mug. "I could go heat it for you if you want."

He grabbed the mug and took a big swig, gulping most of it back in two or three big sips. After setting it down on the desktop, he turned his eyes to me.

In that moment they looked so blue and clear, like water in an undisturbed stream. Grabbing my arms, he pulled me to him with such force it took my breath away.

"I missed you." He said in a low voice, deep and primal from the pit of his belly. He kissed me hard, and my body reacted, my fingers and toes clenching in excitement.

"I'm sorry about yesterday." He said quietly. He leaned his forehead on mine.

"That's cool. My family is having a dinner tonight that you need to come to. This Maritza character will be there."

He started kissing down my neck. "Before that, do you want to go for a ride and park somewhere? We could fool around for a while before the dinner."

Ruh roh. Do I take this as fun and exciting, or should I be worried?

"I thought you said there wasn't enough room to fool around in your car?" I said. His hand slid under my shirt, then into my bra. He started kissing farther down my neckline and I knew where he headed.

"While I very much enjoy this, I don't know if it's a good idea right now. We're at work."

"Mmm. I can't make you scream my name while we're supposed to be working." He leaned down and licked my nipple, squeezing it softly. My breath caught, and I really wanted him to do more.

"I…I…" I could barely form words, a string of excuses for us to leave played through my mind. "I just got here. I can't bail yet. Maybe after lunch?"

He growled, his lips gently touching my neck, the sound rumbling through my body. Pinching my nipple softly as he removed his hand from my shirt, he kissed my lips, gently touching my cheek as he pulled away.

"Later then?" Something in his eyes looked different for a split second, and then it was gone. Trying to ignore the fucky feeling in my stomach, I reached out and touched his cheek.

"Absolutely." Quickly leaving the room, I squeezed out the door and dashed back to my office.

18.

Did I call Meg and accuse her outright of fucking with my boyfriend?

You stupid cow. You can't possibly believe that he's acting like a man who's horny and not a pathetic little boy?

That was it. As usual my stupid brain decided to assume the worst, because God forbid he actually liked me. I bopped my forehead a few times, then an extra two when I realized during my quick exit, I left my coffee in his office.

Now I just needed to find a way to avoid him for a little while, so we didn't do anything dirty at work.

In the P.I business there is always paperwork that needs to be done, so I busied myself with that for as long as I could. Anyone who still believed that this business was all hiding in dark alleys and taking clandestine photos needed to come sit in my office and fill out some forms for an hour.

When my eyes started to feel like they wanted to go

cross eyed I knew I'd done enough. I hesitated, getting up and running back to Eric's office like a puppy wanting to go to the park seemed silly to me. If Ted and Ramona asked where we were going, I'd say out to lunch then let Eric handle it if we didn't return.

Was I really going to blow off work to go have sex with my boyfriend in the middle of the day?

Gathering up my stuff, I straightened my office a bit before grabbing my things and heading to Eric's office. He typed furiously at the computer when I got to the door, his eyes quickly turned when I knocked.

He smiled wide. "Hey. Are you ready to go?"

"Absolutely."

We told the powers that be that we were going out for lunch and made a quick exit. Eric seemed determined, focused. We got in the car, and he sped off.

"Where are we going?" I asked.

"Home." He didn't look at me as he spoke. Not that I would admit it, but I felt relieved he didn't want to go to a park somewhere.

"Wanna hear something weird?" I asked after some time in silence.

"Sure." He finally glanced at me quickly, his eyes remaining forward.

"My cousin Kiera called. Apparently, they have arrested this whore that Jesse was pimping for multiple murders."

"Really? That is weird. Why would she tell you that?"

"They found some of Jesse's personal effects at her

house. She is under the impression this girl could have killed Jesse."

"And did she?"

I eyed him curiously. "My mother's immediate family killed him to jumpstart my prophecy."

"Sure. Ok. But how did they go about doing it?"

I thought about that for a moment. "I have no idea."

"Did you consider the notion that they spelled someone else into doing it? Maybe that's what happened with this girl. *She* was their instrument. But they are still responsible."

I stopped, thinking about what he suggested, "No."

"Well, maybe you should. Either way, they are in the wrong. Not you. I hope you know that." His serious expression never changed, and part of me regretted saying anything to him. What a dumb moment to bring up Jesse.

"Sorry, it was just on my mind. I figured I should mention it, so it wasn't a surprise if it came up at the dinner table." My eyes lowered, and I felt his warm hand reach out for me. Without thinking I grabbed his, holding his one in between my two hands on my lap. His energy felt good as our skin touched, it still hummed with the same vibration from earlier. Any worry faded; the world outside seemed so far away.

In a blink his townhouse appeared, and we parked and gathered our things. The anticipation felt as if I could crack at any moment. Piling my bags neatly by the front door, I carefully took my shoes off and put them on the mat.

Within a minute we were kissing, fumbling at each other's clothes. Buttons came off first; I loved the feel of his bare chest pressed up against mine. Sliding his hands under my butt he lifted me up and pressed me against the wall.

I felt that rumbling growl again as he kissed down my neck and he finally said, "Upstairs or living room?"

"Certainly not the hallway." He linked his hands under my butt as I spoke, and I hung on to him tight as he started up the stairs. Lifting me that far appeared easy and he didn't put me down until he lowered me onto his bed.

He ran his hands over my skin, quickly unhooking my bra. He kissed down my neck, my fingers twining in his hair, and slowly licked around my nipple with the tip of his tongue. I couldn't hold back the moan, and he chuckled as he started pulling my pants down.

"Why is that funny? " I asked, my words barely audible.

"I love how you react to my touch." His hand ran over my body again, this time working its way to removing my clothes, grabbing my panties with his index finger and pulling them down my legs and completely off.

"Hey now." I pushed him back a little. "How come you're not undressed?"

Just as he went to spread my legs he stopped, stood and began unbuckling his pants. I pushed myself back up into a sitting position so I could help. He smiled down at me as I undid his belt buckle and the buttons of his jeans.

Backing up a little, I lay down and pat the bed beside me. He took his pants the rest of the way off then joined me in the bed. Using my right hand, I traced the lines of his pectoral muscles, thin lines of white began to spread up my arms and through my body. I leaned in and kissed him while taking his hardness in my hand. His breathing changed as I began to stroke.

My magic felt as if it seeped out of my hands and into his skin, and it searched for that part of him that previously connected. The last time it happened immediately, now it took a little longer to find it. Once it did it flared like a freshly lit fire, and everything seemed to move into hyper speed.

Every time he touched me, I wanted more. He felt smooth and solid in my hand, like polished stone.

"I love the way you react to me." I said in his ear, continuing to kiss down his neck. He growled again, that low rumble made my toes curl. Quickly he shifted and I lost my grip on him, but now he was on top of me. Our kiss deepened, the warmth of his skin on mine sending a quiet moan from my mouth into his. His hand went down between my legs, where he quickly put one finger inside me, then two. I was ready, the action spreading my wetness, making for easy entry as he moved into me with one fluid thrust.

Condoms immediately flashed through my mind as he idled, and I wondered if I should make him stop to put one on. But everything about it felt *so* right; I took birth control and I trusted him. I'd never done it without a condom before; I'd never trusted anyone enough to.

Eric leaned down and licked my earlobe. "Is this ok?"

"Yeah. I trust you."

He caressed my cheek with one hand, nuzzling into my neck. "You can. I promise."

He thrust into me slowly at first, and I matched every movement with my hips. The spark of our powers melding together felt like they were twisting and braiding, pushing out to our edges. Running my fingers through his hair he kept kissing around my neck and shoulders.

As he picked up his pace a sudden urge washed over me, and I pushed him onto his back and straddled him. He looked up at me surprised, but with a deep passion in his eyes. Grabbing him again, I adjusted myself and put him inside me, moaning as I slid down until he was buried deep. The tips of his fingers dug into my butt cheeks, and he moaned loudly.

Taking his left hand, I intertwined our fingers as I moved my hips back and forth. With his right hand he began massaging my clit as I rode him. My moans grew louder, and he squeezed my hand before sitting up, so he sat on the edge of the bed with me still on him.

We kissed, and he released my hand so he could help guide my hips as I rode him. The other still massaged my tender spot, and my toes curled, and fingers tensed, and I knew I was getting close.

"I want to hear you." His hot breath on my neck made me shiver.

"What?" My thoughts were swimming as I was on the brink.

"*I want to hear you. I want to feel you. I want to know exactly what this does for you.*" He put both his hands on my shoulders; criss crossed over my back and began to push down as he thrust up. He also picked up speed, maybe he was close.

I felt my insides squeeze around him, and we both cried out. The speed pushed me closer and closer, my moans getting so loud I thought I might scream. He did the same, and with one last hard thrust we climaxed together. Clinging tightly to each other, he lay back down, and I went with him, his manhood still inside me.

"Are you ok? " He stroked the back of my head as he spoke.

"Yeah. Are you?" I gently kissed his neck.

"It's ok we didn't..."

"Yeah. I trust you. You're not sleeping with anyone else, right?"

He hugged me. "No, of course not."

"And I'm on birth control. Also not sleeping with anyone else btw."

Rolling me onto my side, I lay my head on his arm as he kissed me. I closed my eyes, a blissful smile spreading across my face.

Is this what love is really like?

When I went to move my head, pain stabbed into my neck, and I cringed. Eric felt my movement; he adjusted me so he could look in my eyes.

He kissed me softly, putting his hand on my neck and his warmth spread into me. That same energy still radiated from his gaze.

"I have to tell you something, and I think you might be mad. But I still have to tell you anyways. I don't want any secrets, especially if things get fucky tonight with Maritza."

Knowing what this confession could do, I seriously considered not doing it. "I know where the demon is."

"Are you responsible for it being in Bliss or did that just happen?"

I pulled back at his statement. "How long have you known?"

"Since the night we got Lemme back. There was a moment when I saw something happen, I wasn't sure what it was at first. I'd never seen a demon possession before, but it was the only thing that made sense. That's why Maritza is around isn't it? Bliss's coven knows something is up, but they can't figure out what."

My eyes lowered. "She claims to actually like Cuddy."

"How could she not?"

"Are you mad?"

He was quiet for a minute, and then said, "No. I wish you would have told me sooner, but no I'm not mad."

"Does Millie know? Or suspect something?"

"Not that I'm aware of." I put my palm over his heart. "For the record, I didn't put *it* in Bliss. I didn't stop it, but I didn't put it in."

"I figured as much." He tilted my chin again towards him, putting his forehead against mine. "If Bliss's coven becomes an issue we'll deal with it. You just have to tell me. Ok? Whatever it is, we face it together. "

I smiled, kissing the tip of his nose. "Together."

19.

We stayed like that for a long time.

I didn't even want to grab a blanket when I felt a little cold, instead I just moved closer to him. Every part of my being wanted to stay like this with him forever, but I knew how disappointed Cuddy and Ted would be if we didn't show up for this dinner.

We went at it once more, this time slower, and with a level of passion I'd never experienced before. It seemed odd to me that I'd been with my previous partner for more than 10 years and it never felt like this.

"What are we telling the boss man we were doing all day?" I asked as we got dressed.

"You didn't text him?" Eric said with a grin.

"No! Jesus fuck, I thought you were taking care of it. Goddammit Eric!" I stopped when I saw him laughing. "What? That's not funny."

"I told him before we left that we were going out on my

assignment for Lewis. We're good."

"The one you fell asleep at the other night?"

"One in the same."

"So, then you better tell me what the assignment is, just to keep our stories straight."

He laughed. "We'll discuss it while we're driving."

Sticking out my bottom lip, I whimpered a little as I walked over to him. "I don't want to go. I want to stay here."

"I think Ted would be more upset if we missed dinner with the happy couple than us missing work." He tapped my outstretched lip with his finger, laughing at my expression. "And the weekend is coming up. We could do this all weekend, if you'd like."

My pout turned into a grin. "Oh, I very much like. Do you think you'd be up for it?"

"Absolutely." He took my face in his hands, kissing my lips. "We'll just have to stock up on supplies."

"Supplies?"

"Like food, Gatorade, you know." He laughed as he pulled me into a hug. "Now let's go before I change my mind."

Chris Lewis assigned Eric the job I wasn't able to complete. Only now there were names and faces he kept an eye on, which meant Eric spent more time at Ren than I would like.

Eric shrugged me off when I mentioned it. "Ninety percent of the time I am sitting outside in my car. And I told you, you can trust me."

"It's not you I don't trust." I said flatly. "Maybe we should go see Moira and get you protection from Meg's powers. And Shae made those comments about Lewis."

"You're not worried about angry drug dealers?"

I chuckled. "From what I saw of them? No. Not at all. But October Daniels has some connection to Bliss. October helped dispose of Lucia Kinkaid's body."

"Noted." He smiled and nodded as we turned on to my street. "Are you ready for this?"

I spotted Maritza's little black sports car parked beside Ted's and I cringed.

"Maybe Poppy will be home. That would make it much more interesting."

"Hello!" I called out when we came inside. Some thumping, then Cuddy stuck his head out from the kitchen.

"Oh good! You're here!" his face lit up like a kid on Christmas. A female giggled from somewhere in the house, Eric and I briefly made eye contact.

"I wouldn't miss it for the world, Cuddy." I kissed him on the cheek, passing by him towards the living room. "Is Poppy here?"

"Fuck no. Dad gave her fifty bucks and told her to go away." He shifted awkwardly as he spoke. "Sorry. Gotta go."

"Cas! You got my favorite nephew in law with you?" Ted yelled out from the living room. "Get some beer and come in here. Bring me one too."

I turned back to Cuddy to ask him to pass me a few out of the fridge but before I could Ted yelled, "My son is concerned we will get drunk and embarrass him!"

"It wouldn't be a Bishop family gathering if we didn't." Grabbing three beers, I handed one to Eric as we headed for the living room.

Ted sat in his chair, and Maritza sat cross legged on the floor a few feet away from him. My uncle looked happier than I'd seen him in a long time; his big silly grin made me wonder if Cuddy's nervousness was warranted.

Maritza took one look at us, and her eyes widened, the glyph on her wrist flashed white for an instant. I smiled big. We left being naked for this. It better be amusing at the very least.

"Whoa! Camille! When did you get the tattoo?" Ted exclaimed, pointing at my arm.

"Oh." Looking down at my arm, I'd forgotten to cover it. "Right. I did that recently."

"It's very cool." Ted yanked my arm over to him so he could get a closer look. "Why the sword?"

"It's Excalibur."

He paused, taking a minute to process. "Your Mom would have dug that."

"I hope so." Kissing the top of his head, I handed him a beer before sitting on the couch next to Eric.

"Maritza was just asking why we call him Cuddy." Ted said.

"You know, it's been so long I don't even remember." I took a swig of my beer.

"I know his mother hated it."

I chuckled. "I'm sure that was one of the reasons we kept doing it."

Ted laughed and didn't say anything.

"He was really little. I think it was around the same time he called me Cas for the first time. He had trouble speaking at first, and he probably said something like Cuddy when he talked about himself, and we just went with it."

"He's not said much about his mom…." Maritza began.

I shrugged. "And he won't unless you have to meet her. She's a grade A piece of work."

"Cas." Ted warned.

"What? I didn't say the C word." I raised my hands in defeat. "So is Cuddy actually cooking or what's happening?"

"Hey now. My son can cook! Just you wait and see." Ted proclaimed.

"So, we're eating a lavish meal of pizza pockets and popcorn?"

"Have a little faith, Camille."

"We're actually doing cooking and nutrition as part of our Phys Ed curriculum." Maritza chimed in. "He's learned a few things."

Ted stood slowly, not quite swaying, mumbling he needed to take a leak and promptly left the room. Eric put his hand on my back protectively as I turned towards Maritza.

"I'm happy to inform you that your info checked out, and *mi reina* does not feel she needs to speak with you on the matter."

I laughed. "So why are you still here?"

She kept her gaze locked with mine. "Because I actually care for Christian."

"Before I begin, Eric meet Maritza, one of them *bruja* coven bitches. Maritza, the Merlin." I pointed back and forth between the two of them. "You seem genuine. So, we're cool for now. But you must give me your word that if something happens and I am not here, you will protect them. Can you do that?"

She smiled. "Absolutely."

"They know *nothing* about any of this and I would like to keep it that way."

"Understood. And for the record I'm sorry about what Bliss did."

"Thanks. Me too."

But am I sorry for what I did to Bliss?

Sorry, not sorry.

Cuddy made one of the best chicken with mixed vegetables and rice dishes I'd ever eaten. Ted looked so proud I couldn't stop smiling.

Once everything finished and cleaned up, we said goodbye to Maritza and the boys went off to do other things while I said bye to Eric.

"You could stay you know." I told him as I played with the collar of his jacket. We stood on the porch; the air started getting a bit cold.

He kissed me, pulling me into his arms. It felt like a quick kiss but with so much feeling. When I looked into his eyes that same hunger still shone out.

"I'll see you tomorrow." He kissed me one last time then walked to his car.

"Let me know you got home ok!" I called out before he got in. He nodded in agreement, waving as he drove away.

When I got back inside, Ted and Cuddy were both asleep in the living room. Ted in his chair, and Cuddy on the couch. I covered them both with throw blankets we kept on one end of the couch.

Once in my room, I put my phone on my bed so I could see when Eric called, and I summoned the sword.

My phone beeped with a text from Millie, asking if I found Eric. I let her know I did, and he'd been working late, and that I would call her tomorrow. It felt weird not telling her about the sword, but it would involve more questions than I cared to answer at the moment.

Standing on my area rug, I practiced holding and slashing with the sword. I'd dealt with some weapons in my life; coming from a family of law enforcement, we were taught to have a healthy respect and fear of the power a weapon can hold. But those were generally guns. My Uncle Don and Cousin Benny carried boot knives, but they were narcotics officers, so it came with the territory.

It felt like something I needed to attune myself to, something that should become an extension of my physical form. If it truly was *my sword*.

After doing this for a little while, I sat crossed legged on the carpet with the sword laid across my knees. Closing my eyes and taking a breath, I tried to meditate for the first time.

The benefits of meditating were pushed on me for ages.

In the years after my parents died, a laundry list of therapists attempted to teach me as a way to help alleviate my anxiety, but I could not quiet my mind long enough for it to ever work.

But something happened when I sat down. Maybe the energy from the sword played into it, I'm not sure, but my mind just opened.

A wave of calm washed over me as if the world around stopped. It felt different than the whole out in the woods alone scenario, it seemed closer to floating in space. Part of me liked the nothing. Too much shit went on in my fucked up little world for me not to love a little silence.

Another beep from my phone brought me out of my trance. Opening my eyes, I flicked my wrist and the sword disappeared. Something inside me felt more in sync. Like I could take on challenges on my own and keep standing.

Not surprising Eric finally arrived home; he said he was exhausted and going to bed. Quickly acknowledging, I did the same, telling him I would see him at work tomorrow.

After a happy morning with the boys, we arrived at work all smiles. And I continued to smile, watching the clock for when I heard Eric come in. We were one step closer to the weekend, one step closer to the alone time I so craved.

While I waited, I used a secret code Q got us to access Shae Rielle's personnel file. Ted said she'd been a cop a long time; surely there would be something I could learn about her.

Listed as her emergency contact was the name Otrera Firefly. The file referred to her as her domestic partner. Given the date that Shae started, they'd been together it least 20 years.

Shae came up around the same time as my dad and Uncle Ted. Surely that meant she would be well acquainted with my father's former partner, Dorien Reid. Funny that she said Chris Lewis wasn't good but not a word about Reid.

Her arrest record was high. Well respected and intelligent, on paper she would make a good mentor for Kiera.

She operated in a world that I knew quite well, which meant it could be a way we relate to each other.

When I looked at the clock again it was almost noon. And no Eric.

Grabbing my phone, I skipped the text and called him. The phone rang and rang until his machine picked up; I hung up rather than leaving a message.

A quick hop over my desk and I went to talk to Ramona.

"Hey, is Eric here yet?" I asked Ramona.

"No hunny. Maybe you should call him." Ramona replied without looking up. Quickly thanking her, I dashed to the end of the hall to Chris Lewis's office.

Knocking and immediately opening the door, Chris looked shocked to see me. He sat in his big desk chair, hunched over some papers.

"Got any ideas where Eric is?" I asked him.

"Lost track of your boyfriend already?" He chuckled to himself. Mashing my hands into my pockets, I bit the inside of my lip to stop myself from lashing out.

"I figured since he's been sitting in a car outside your strip club you might know why he hasn't shown up for work yet."

"He wasn't there at my direction. I don't know what he told you." Chris looked briefly at me than returned to his papers. "And reign in that moxy at the office."

Bowing, I closed the door behind me.

"What's up Cas?" Ted called out to me as I tried to bolt past his doorway.

"I can't find Eric." I stood by his doorframe but didn't look at him.

"Maybe he's still asleep." Ted stopped typing. "Don't do that."

"Do what?"

"He's not Jesse, Camille. Don't treat him like he is. I am sure it's innocent."

I smiled, but I knew the expression looked weak. "I am sure it is."

Going back to my office, I tried to sit and do some work. Do *something* other than compulsively worry about where he was and what he was doing. I could hear Ted and Chris walking around and talking, my paranoid mind began to twist and turn. I became convinced they talked about me, about how stupid I was, how childish. That I could never do anything 'normal'. More hours went by as I stewed in my own shit.

I opened the tracking software on my laptop and typed in his phone number. Staring at the start button, thoughts ran through my mind a million miles a minute. In my very core I knew Eric wasn't like Jesse. But something itched at the back of my mind.

Why would he lie about Chris when he knew I could just ask him? Or Chris lied?

Fuck it.

Going through this kind of behaviour for so long made it part of who I am. It would take time to learn something else. I couldn't erase so many years of bullshit in a few weeks.

Pushing the button didn't make me feel guilty one bit. Eric lied to me. And now he's missing in action. I needed to know what was going on.

Within a minute a blip appeared. A bright yellow spot appeared downtown, close to the entertainment district. It blipped three times, and then went off.

Without thinking I wrote down the location, and then took a photo of my computer screen of exactly where it stopped. Then I waited, hoping it was some sort of glitch.

Nope.

The blip never came back.

There were not enough cuss words that I could string together to express my emotion.

Grabbing my phone, I called Millie.

"Something's wrong." I said when she answered.

"What do you mean?" she asked.

"Eric never showed up for work. He lied to me about what he's been doing when he disappeared before, and not even a good lie. I just tracked his phone, and the little light flashed like three times then stopped. And has not started back up and that was like 10 minutes ago." I blurted out; any signs I'd been annoyed with her completely gone.

"Could something be wrong with the software?"

"No. I checked."

"Could he be with another girl?"

I huffed. "Fuck you, Millie." I hung up. Tension started to build in my neck, as I slowly moved it around to try to loosen it more pain began to build in a new spot. I needed help and I needed it fast, and I didn't have a lot of options.

Trying Eric's phone one more time, I prayed to a deity I didn't believe in that I overreacted. Still no answer. This time I left a message.

"Hey, it's Camille. I don't know where you are, but please call me." I hung up before I started to cry. My options at this point were limited. Either I went on my own, saving myself some embarrassment if it turns out to be nothing; or I called Millie back and sucked up, so they went with me, and potentially dealt with Ledo's stupidness; or I called Lorcan Fitzpatrick and told him he owed me; or I lied to Ted and asked him to drop me off. None of them were ideal; going alone caused the least amount of blowback.

Packing my things slowly and methodically forced me to the realization that I could not go on my own. Sucking in my tattered pride, I called Millie back.

"That was low of me. I apologise." She said when she answered.

"Hey, you might be right. And I'd rather you witness my epic embarrassment than risk walking into something unprepared." *But you are prepared, meat head. You have the fucking sword.*

She chuckled. "I'll pick you up in 20 minutes."

"Are you alone?"

"No."

"Balls."

"Hey now, the boy has been instructed to be on his best behaviour. You need to be as well. Besides, Nya can stand in between you." I heard Nya's voice protesting in the background.

I exhaled loudly, not even realizing I'd been holding in breath. "Fine. See you shortly."

Ted prepared to leave as I went to talk to him.

"You ok?" he asked when my head popped in the doorway. "Still nothing from him, huh?"

"I will be. I'm sure he's fine. But Millie is coming to pick me up, so I am heading out. I finished up any work lying around and since I don't have any clients at the moment, I thought it might be ok. Day is almost done anyhow." It took Ted putting a hand on my shoulder for me to look at him. I used every bit of strength I had not to burst into tears.

"Hey, just relax. Go have fun. I am sure he'll turn up." He kissed me on the forehead, and I turned tail and dashed out of the building to Millie's waiting SUV.

20.

"So where is it?" Ledo held nothing back when I got in the vehicle.

I unfolded the map I'd printed out and pointed at the little star. Millie nodded in acknowledgment and started driving. Leaning to one side I rested my head against the cool glass of the door.

"Where's what?" I grumbled.

"The sword. I know you have it." Ledo's voice felt like a cheese grater on my nerves.

"If I did, don't you think it would be a bad idea to piss me off right now?" I checked his expression in the rear-view mirror. Regulating my breathing took a lot of work.

"Nya, can you scry for Eric?" Millie asked.

"What's that?" I said.

"It's the magic equivalent of a tracking device. Sort of." Nya replied. "Now shut up for a minute and I will see."

"Why didn't you tell me you could do that?" I whispered

to Millie.

"You could do it too if you bothered to listen." She smiled as she spoke. "I'm glad you called. I have had a weird feeling about him for a while."

"Oh! That reminds me. They have arrested someone for Jesse's murder. Not le Fay."

Millie's eyebrows rose. "Oh?"

"Could they have spelled someone into becoming a killer?"

"What do you mean?"

"Well, the girl that Jesse was pimping. Turns out she's a black widow killer or something like that. And they found some of his belongings at her house. But Harold and his family told me they killed him. Could they set it up to make it look like this girl did it?"

She looked shocked. "They could, but I couldn't imagine they were smart enough to pull that off. It's a lot more work than you might think."

"Have you heard anything about them lately?"

"No." Millie looked back at her children, and they both shook their heads no. The action seemed a bit rehearsed.

"I got a hit on Eric." Nya's eyes now looked totally white, her pupils and irises glazed over. "He's in a dark room, looks like a basement. There is someone there, but I can't see their face."

"Does it look like he's in trouble?" I asked.

"I can't tell. He has a weird expression on his face."

The tension in my neck flared up again. Grabbing my pill bottle out of my pocket I dry swallowed two Percocet's.

Pushing up my sleeves, my hands were bright almost glowing white and pulsing like some kind of crazy beacon.

"New tattoo?" Millie asked before I could hide my arm.

"Yeah." I flashed it to Ledo. "That's the only sword I got."

As the white pushed up my forearms it stung and throbbed, making me flinch in pain. Millie watched me curiously. Once the pain dulled, they became itchy, and I felt the tips of my fingers digging in a little too much.

"How many of those painkillers are you taking a day?" Millie asked me quietly.

I smiled. "Not enough."

"Camille."

"One thing at a time, goddammit. Are we almost there?" Looking outside my window, we were a few blocks away from Chinatown and where we parked to go to Madam Vo's. The streets were empty, everything moist from a recent rainfall.

Millie parked out front of a three-story red brick semi detached house with rows of similar looking places around it. Everything smelled like wet dirt. Nya got out and did her little trick with the parking machine ticket while I stashed my laptop in Millie's trunk.

Once the doors were shut and locked the four of us stood on the sidewalk and looked around. The rumbling of a streetcar going by a few blocks away made the ground feel like it shook. Everything seemed dingy, even the plants. As if someone painted this landscape with a wash of brown paint.

"Where to now, boss?" Nya asked me.

"I don't know. The software wasn't specific. The scry didn't show anything?"

"Nope, just basement. Concentrate on him and his power, and what it feels like to you, and maybe you can sense him."

I closed my eyes and concentrated on Eric. His smile, his eyes, the warm feeling when he touched my skin. His energy.

Something of him prickled on my skin, faint and gently tickling along my edges. In my mind I could see an alley, brightly colored graffiti surrounding me.

"There's something but its weak." I said aloud.

"Could he be blocking?" Ledo asked.

"He's a Merlin. If he blocked, we wouldn't find him." I didn't hide my distaste for him. Ledo's presence and my annoyance kept me motivated, the faster I got away from him the better. The way he looked at our surroundings, his repulsion quite clear, made me contemplate punching him more than once.

The hint of Eric stretched out to me again. His magic knew me and attempted to attach itself, the bond that we'd formed while being intimate extending to our powers. Everything inside me reached out for him like an octopus tentacle and latched on to what I could.

But it felt weak, like it started to fade.

I opened my eyes, pointed at the fourth house in a row and said, "This way."

As we started forward the front door of the house

opened, and a dark head peered out, looked around, and quickly retreated back inside.

"Is there something you all can cast so they don't know we're coming?" I asked.

"You realize you're going above and beyond for a dude who's probably just boning another chick, right?" Ledo tried to laugh but Nya punched him in the shoulder before he could. Turning to him, I got right up in his face.

"Fine. Ok. Sure. He's cheating on me. Let's go walk into that public embarrassment, and you can watch as your mother and sister stop me from committing murder. *Again.*" Smiling big with teeth, I pivoted and continued towards the house. Logic brain told me to hold off and make a plan, but the devil on my shoulder said they already knew we were here the second we pulled up, it's too late to prepare now. So go kick the door in and get your man.

Stomping my way up the rickety wood steps, I got a whiff of something warm and metallic as soon as I reached for the door. Trying the knob, it didn't budge.

Concentrating on the lock, I twisted it again as hard as I could and it snapped, turning fully and opening. Stepping through the doorway I stopped and listened, everyone else pausing behind me.

"Is that blood?" Ledo whispered loudly, sniffing the air. "I am so not prepared for a fight."

"Then go wait in the car, wussy." Nya snapped at him. I wanted to high five her, but it seemed inappropriate at the moment.

"You two are like a bunch of little kids. Shut your

traps, we need to find Eric." Millie didn't bother whispering but didn't yell either, just spoke in that forceful Mom voice that made it clear she wasn't messing around.

Following where my magic directed, we began walking through the rundown house. Furniture lay in pieces, falling apart and dirty, with rugs so filthy and crusted with dirt it almost looked made of mud. The smell of unwashed bodies and rot filled the room, with the overtone of metallic and burning plastic that seemed to establish residence in your nostrils. Boxes with tin cans full of cigarette butts and other smoking paraphernalia littered the room. It reminded me of the crack house we found Bucky's phone in so long ago.

Wow. If Bucky could see Bliss now, I wonder what he would say? Maybe I should ask Maritza about their involvement in his death.

We got to the kitchen in the back and saw no signs of life on this floor. Tempted to split us up to cover more ground, I opened my mouth to suggest it when I heard a noise coming from beneath us.

I leaned over and whispered to Millie. "Check out the back door and see if there is another entrance to the basement from outside."

She nodded, and quietly crept out the broken screen to take a look while I stood in front of the tall thin door that I assumed led to the basement. Millie quickly returned, letting me know what I'd already suspected.

Only one way in and one way out.

"Nya, you and Ledo can stay up here and guard the door." I told her quietly.

"And let you and my mom walk into the lion's den alone? No thank you." She shook her head. "I'll take my chances with you."

I made eye contact with Ledo for the first time in a while. Before I could say anything he said, "And let you get my family killed? Fuck off with that shit."

"He could be down there having an orgy." I said to no one in particular.

Millie put a hand on my shoulder. By the look in her eyes, I knew she thought the same thing I did. "Let's hope so."

The smell of blood grew stronger as we descended down the basement stairs. I went first, Millie behind me, Nya and Ledo took up the rear. Luckily the staircase itself wasn't too treacherous and I made it down without falling. The wood felt rickety, only made worse by the weight of four adults. The unfinished railing almost gave me splinters.

When we reached the bottom, one overhead light bulb hung from a string, swinging in the middle of the room, casting a strange light over the scene in front of us.

The floor looked like dirt, which explained the state of the upstairs. My eyes immediately went to the back wall. Bodies hung shackled about six feet high to the cinderblocks. The light made it difficult to make out any of them, but I did catch a glimpse of what looked like a very dead Tobias Kinkaid, blood covering the front of his body.

In the middle of the room strapped to a chair sat my sweet Eric, his head leaned to one side. He looked unconscious, thankfully. Cuts ran up his arms and a strange symbol covered over his heart, scratched in with what looked like the tip of a very sharp object.

With her back turned to us, a woman teetered in big plastic heels close to the back wall. She wore a lime green thong bikini and her dark hair piled in a massive beehive on top of her head.

"Millie." I said quietly.

"Yeah?" She whispered.

"I think I know where the demon went."

Hearing that phrase, the woman turned around, Bliss's maniacal smile made me cringe.

"I was hoping you would come."

21.

"Let him go." I growled between clenched teeth.

"I told you when I took this body, *blanchmains*. I want *power*. This man has the power I need." Pointing towards Eric, Bliss's voice sounded dark and twisted as it spoke the demon's words.

"You knew it was in Bliss's body?" Millie snapped. "I asked you! Repeatedly!"

"And you would have thought I put it there and *I didn't!* I just didn't stop it from happening!" I yelled back. "But that's a fight for another time!"

"WE should leave you here to deal with the mess you created!"

"I didn't create it! We can summon my mother right now and you can shit on her about it. All of this," I made a big circling hand gesture, "is on the genius who wanted to bind my powers."

The demon twitched, a strange clicking noise coming

from its mouth. "The ritual is already begun, *blanchmains*. You cannot stop it now. You just have to watch the Merlin die."

"Back up guys." I barked at my people, and as I tried to level my breathing, sparks shooting out of my fingertips. My magic began to swirl inside me, including this new part that felt like live electricity shooting through my hand.

My sword hand is singing.

"This must have been what was off about him." Millie told me. "It must have latched on to him somehow. Did you guys encounter it recently?"

"I had to go to Ren for fucking Lorcan Fitzpatrick." My eyes never left the demon. "Is that when you did it? When my back was turned?"

It cackled. "Surprise!"

"Take me instead. Let him go. I won't fight you." I told it calmly.

It laughed again. "You're a terrible liar."

"Alright. Fine. I'm going to gut you like a fish. Then, if you manage to survive and one of those bodies is actually Tobias Kinkaid, they're going to destroy you. And I am going to laugh my ass off as I watch you burn."

It went to move forward, and I mirrored its movements. Holding out my hand, I sent out my power and latched into this *thing* inside Bliss's body and tried to pull it out. The demon continued to laugh, a hideous bird like cackle that sounded nothing like the body it currently inhabited.

"You need blood magic." I heard Lilly's voice like a whisper in my head. I blinked and she appeared beside me, no weird eye thing this time.

"I don't know any." I said, Millie asked me from behind who I was talking to.

"You have to draw blood. Any blood while you are performing the ritual. Do what you would normally do but draw blood while you do it." Lilly directed.

"Millie!" I yelled, my eyes never leaving the demon. "What do I do?"

She sobbed in the back, her voice cracking with pain. "I don't know."

The demon broke free from my tether, knocking me back a few feet. It laughed again, the sound rung off the walls like a loud gong and we were forced to cover our ears.

"Lilly says I need blood magic." I told Millie.

"No. You can't do that to yourself." Millie said. "*He would not want you to do that to yourself for him.*"

"I won't let him die like this!" I screamed at her. A surge went through my body; unsure if it was magic, or energy, or just my blood, I knew I needed to act fast.

Standing up, I screamed as loud as I could. It reverberated through the room like a shock wave, sending everyone flying back. It pushed Eric on the chair against the wall, but not hard enough to knock him free. Paying little attention to the other's behind me, I advanced on the demon. Wiggling my fingers and flicking my wrist, I summoned the sword.

Gripping the handle with the blade pointed down, I started forward. She attempted to swing at me, and I used my left arm to block it. Punching forward with the sword, I slashed at her stomach. Blood began to seep from the wound.

The demon ran its well-manicured fingers through the red. It licked the tips, like a kid licking something sweet off its fingers.

"You'll have to do better than that this time." It said with a grin. In a blink it came at me, luckily I moved fast enough to toss it off and send it flying at the wall.

"You can't just kill it. You have to banish it." Lilly said. "Remember that spell I taught you for your ex-boyfriend? That should work."

"Got it. " Back in my fighting stance, I could hear Millie's pleas in the background. I couldn't even look at Eric right now, I needed to focus on the task at hand.

I had to save him.

22.

I dove at the demon, punching it in the face with my sword hand. It stumbled back, confused, and I knocked her feet out from under her and she fell flat on her back. The disorientation gave me enough time to straddle her and pin her down. Thrashing, it scratched my cheek with its stupid nails, and I punched it again. Putting my free hand over its face, I pushed down as I used the sword to make a small cut into my wrist.

"Blood of my blood, bring forth the power only my life-force can wield." I proclaimed. The demon began to fight harder; clearly it knew what came next. Millie's screams got louder, but none of them came closer to try to stop me.

With the tip of my pointer finger, I dipped it in blood and smeared it across the demon's forehead. "Take this wretched creature back to the bowels of darkness from whence it came. Break it's tether to this mortal coil, and this realm."

The demon started laughing again. "You're too late!"

Its sing song voice made me push harder.

"Blood of my blood, send this demon back to hell! " I yelled, pushing my power down at it, latching on to every piece I could feel within Bliss's body.

I sensed something else in there, a little glimmer of white light that could only be the last spark of my former friend. It cried out to me, I could feel it's deep and consuming pain.

But then the blackness snuffed it out. I knew in that moment Bliss was gone. She would not be coming back from this.

Gut punching sadness rushed through me, and I screamed for her, screamed for the mistakes we both made. We'd been friends once, or so I'd thought, but beyond all that she was a person. But this life never gave her a proper chance. It never gave any of us a proper chance.

The blackness began to bubble up like lava. Now that it took complete control of Bliss's body, it pooled itself around any connection I made and crawled inside it. When I looked down at my hand, the blood turned black and crawled up my skin like a snake.

"Fight back, dumbass!" Lilly yelled at me.

"I am in control." I lowered my face down so I could growl in the demon's ear. "You will not take him. Do you understand? "

"No, but I could take you." The demon suddenly jumped, knocking me back and into the wall, where I slid down until I sat flat on my ass.

"Ow! That hurt!" I screamed at it. Without even standing I sent those magic threads out of my hands, and they latched on to every living thing in the room. A thicker longer one came out of my sword hand and went straight into the demon's chest. The slash I'd made earlier now oozed black liquid.

"I will have his powers, *blanchmains*." The demon growled at me. "And then I will take yours and your little team over there. You're not strong enough to stop me. "

This is it, bitch. Do or die time.

You either go whole hog, or let the damn thing kill you right now because you know you would never be able to live with yourself if it killed Eric. Might as well go down swinging.

How long have people been kicking you for?

How long are you just going to take this bullshit before you fucking rise?

You're supposed to be all powerful.

Be powerful.

ENOUGH GAMES.

Standing up, I could feel lightning sparking from my fingertips. Energy surged from the sword and the threads sparked to life, I heard my friends cry out in pain. Wrapping the one connected to the demon around my fingers, I pulled as hard as I could.

It sputtered, coughing and laughing. I tugged again. Black liquid dripped from its eyes like tears, with little spots at the corner of its mouth. Quickly I shot across the room, my hand flying over its mouth.

"Blood of my blood, I banish you from this plane. I release you from your mortal coil, never to return." My voice didn't sound like my own, a guttural growl raspier than I'd ever heard. The black ooze began to flow up my arm and into the cut I'd made on my wrist.

"Blood of my blood, leave this place and never return." I looked deep in its eyes as I spoke the final words, and then plunged Excalibur into its stomach all the way to the hilt.

A loud snap and crackle and I flung back, slamming hard enough into the wall that I saw stars. As I slid down to the ground my body went heavy, and I lost consciousness.

23.

Bliss's body lay on the floor a few feet away from me, discarded like a leftover husk from when you shuck an ear of corn.

Black ooze seeped from my hands as it crawled into my veins, demon blood becoming one with mine. It puddled around Bliss and in random spots on the floor.

My memory felt shrouded with fog, the hit on the head combined with the pain in my neck really shaking me up. But I did know that I saved him. Before the demon could overtake him, I pulled it back and *I saved him.*

A pulse radiated out of Bliss's body, and it caused my powers to hum under my skin. A new feeling since the demon blood went into my system, a new dimension to my powers. Everything about me felt more alive, like I could feel every tiny hair and skin cell on my body.

Squeezing the muscles in my left hand I could feel Bliss's body twitch and move, the bones contorting as it forced itself to stand. It teetered on unstable feet like a newborn horse, looking ridiculous in her coordinating neon green bra and panties and clear plastic stripper shoes. Black goo smeared across her stomach and around her mouth, dripping down her chin. Her blank, dead eyes turned to me, waiting for command. Power radiated from the pommel of the sword that I clutched tightly in my right hand.

"My God, Camille. What have you done?" Millie's voice shocked me back to reality. I turned to see her and Ledo hunched over Nya's body, Millie watched me in horror as Ledo attempted to revive his sister.

"I had to save him." My words were barely audible. Dashing across the room, I used the sword to cut Eric free. He flopped into my arms; I could faintly feel his heartbeat.

Above us I heard a bunch of noise, but I ignored it. Placing my hand on the symbol on Eric's chest, a warm white light cast a glow from my hand over it until it disappeared. His eyes shot open, and he looked up at me.

"You came." He whispered.

"Of course I did, what did you think was going to happen?" I laughed, tears streaming down my cheeks. He sat up and looked around, jumping a little when he saw zombie Bliss.

"It's ok. The demon is gone." Stroking his hair, his eyes took in the scene around the room.

Something came thundering down the stairs and I covered him protectively. Three figures with masks, one smaller than the others, came down the stairs. The two bigger figures carried guns, which were pointed at us. Even in the black outfits I could make out a feminine shape to the smaller one.

"Status update, Sparrow." A radio crackled. The woman lifted her hand and a pink energy bolt shot out, smacking right into zombie Bliss and it fell into a heap, my connection lost. They turned to us as their third went and cut one of the men off the wall. When his body hit the floor, I caught a better glimpse of Tobias Kinkaid's battered face. They spoke quickly to each other in a language I didn't understand, the voice another clear indicator that the smallest of the three was female.

"Hey, we don't want any trouble. We're here on a rescue mission, just like you." I raised my hands above my head, flicking my wrist and the sword disappeared.

The woman came closer as her companions picked up the lifeless body of Tobias Kinkaid and began to leave.

"Tu es blanchmains?" She asked me in perfect French. The black mask looked solid, smooth, with tinted glass over the eyes. Its face came to a bit of a point, like the Venetian plague doctor mask but more bird like.

Like a Sparrow.

"Yes, I am." I tried to sit up tall and look brave, staring at the masked face. Not being able to see their eyes when someone spoke felt unsettling.

She giggled, and when one of her partners called *Sparrow* from upstairs, she turned and left.

Looking at the others, Nya sat up and stared around

the room in a daze. Millie cried, and Ledo glared around angrily.

"You did it." Lilly's voice said in my mind. "I didn't think you had it in you."

I looked around for her. "I had to save him."

"We have to get out of here." Millie said, looking down at Nya. "Can you walk?"

The young woman nodded, and they pulled her up to standing. Millie let Nya lean on her brother for a minute and came over to Eric to help me pull him up.

"Who are they?" Nya called out, pointing across the room. Stepping away from Eric, I approached the back wall.

Pointing to the one I recognized. "That one I believe is Tobias Kinkaid's personal bodyguard. The other two I don't know."

"We should go, before they come back." Millie helped Eric take a step. They all went up the stairs first and I followed along behind.

When I got to the top of the steps, I stared down at the mangled corpse of Bliss Fiori, which looked like a marionette when their strings aren't pulled. The part of me that would feel something for her no longer existed. As a wise woman once said, she made her bed. She could go fuck herself in it. The new me rose from this horror show better, faster, and stronger.

I looked down at my arms, surprised to see that the white now mixed with patches of black in a weird almost Jackson Pollock like paint splatter.

"Hands up!" A female voice said from behind me, I heard

a gun cock. "Put them behind your head!"

Fuck.

Slowly I turned on my heel, taking one step up into the open doorway. Moving out of the patch of darkness the woman holding the gun took me by surprise.

"You a cop?" I asked.

"No. Something much worse." Her steady hand kept the gun pointed at my head. "The demon still down there?"

"No. I banished it." I gestured to the talisman around her neck. "You get that from Moira?"

She hesitated, no sign the familiar name threw her off. "Why?"

"I saw your photo on her wall. It was an old photo, mind you, but it most definitely was you. You were a teenager maybe?" I thought about asking about the child I saw her on the bus with, but she may take that as a threat.

"Anyone left down there?" She asked.

"Someone already came for Tobias Kinkaid. But three others and what's left of the demon's mortal body." It felt weird to not refer to Bliss like an actual person.

"Alright."

"I'm going to go now with my friends. You may have seen them leave." We slid around each other, leaving some distance in between, her gun and my hands still up. "My name is Camille Bishop. I'm the *blanchmains*. What's your name?"

"Frost. Kennedy Frost." She gestured with her gun towards the exit. "I'd leave now if I were you."

"Gladly." I turned away from her and headed for the door, not looking back.

Millie waited on the sidewalk for me, Eric sat in the back seat with the door open, looking like he wanted to bolt. Jogging once I got off the front steps, I caught up with them quickly.

"Everything ok?" Millie asked.

"Yeah. Let's get the hell out of here." I climbed in the back seat beside Eric, who immediately took my hand.

As Millie put the car in gear, a series of loud bangs startled us all, with smashing glass and loud thumping. The boarded up-front window of the house we just exited exploded, flashes of hot red and orange shot out as the house burst into flames.

Watching out the back window, I waited to see if someone, *anyone* ran out of that house. Even though I saw no one, I knew that wouldn't be the last time I saw Kennedy Frost.

No one said a word, they probably assumed I rigged the explosion, and I wouldn't correct them. Trying to explain the strange line of coincidences that made up Kennedy Frost would only make them paranoid.

Kissing the top of Eric's hand, I felt complete with him beside me. Deep in my soul I knew I did the right thing. I saved him, and that was everything. Maybe fate brought me here, and that was just fine.

Kennedy Frost

2001.

Even in the early spring, it felt cold when darkness fell. Not to the bone, but cold enough that you really needed a jacket. The ground still carried some of the mess of winter, flowers not quite poking their way up to freedom. A time of rebirth.

Windsor told us to be prepared, so when he called mentioning a job, I was ready. But if you knew me, like *really* knew me, you'd know I tried my best to prepare for anything and everything.

I kept my black jacket zipped up tight and all the pockets closed so nothing could fall out. Not that I carried much, no ID, only some cash, a burner phone, and my kit. My little box of goodies contained a lot more than my fellow recruits. I wouldn't take the chance of not being prepared so I always came with a little of everything.

Wiggling my fingers at my side, Jack took it as a signal and held my hand. He never prepared. Jack somehow always managed to kick ass while flying by the seat of his pants. I hoped one day his mellowness would rub off on me.

Tonight, his eyes glowed in a way that sent my anxiety flying off the rails. He was scared but would never vocalize it.

I couldn't blame him.

I was scared too.

After our last hunt he'd be stupid not to be. We lost three people that day. But his arrogance would eventually take over, and he would keep going just to prove a point. And I would go with him. I would never let him go alone. Like a lovesick fool, I would follow him into the dark.

Windsor waited by the front door with the others. Well, what remained of our group of recruits.

Almost half of us were gone.

"Bout time you two showed up." Windsor growled at us. He dressed a little less like a stoned professor today, the logos of his Eddie Bauer windbreaker clearly visible. If you looked down the back of his neck, you'd probably find the price tag still attached.

"You could have started without us...oh right! You don't have the *balls*." I would not deal with his attitude towards us any longer. I was sick and tired of *him*. His bullshit demeanour and unpleasant disposition made me hate his presence in any situation.

"Watch your mouth, Frost." The older and larger Windsor closed the space between us, getting right in my face. His breath smelled minty, the freshness overriding anything that could pass as cologne.

I pulled my gun, so fast he couldn't react, and pushed the tip of the barrel into his forehead. "If *anyone* else dies, and I mean anyone, I have a bullet with your name on it."

"Is that a threat?"

I ground the gun in harder. "More like an FYI."

"So how many?" Jack asked, pushing my hand gently away from Windsor's face.

"A dozen. Maybe fifteen." Windsor scowled at me as he backed away. "Should be a piece of cake."

"That's what you said last time and there were *more*. How can we trust you?" I asked. I let Jack step between me and our handler, if I could even call him that at this point. He didn't really 'handle' us; he gave up any guise of caring for us long ago and mostly barked orders and directions like a pathetic excuse for a commander. At some point, we'd be in the position to contradict him and that would change *everything*.

"I have been watching this place all night, Frost. If you don't want to trust me it's your call." Windsor pulled Destiny over; she'd been in the shadows when we approached. "Desi has been here too. She can tell you."

Bile began to rise up in my throat when I looked at Destiny. He used her like a meat shield, his claws firmly sunk into the skin on her shoulder like an active wear clad demon. Hearing him say her nickname made it feel dirty. Anything he touched he seemed to taint. But Desi's expression said it all – she knew too. Something wasn't right.

"The one who killed Amir is in there." Destiny's eyes grew dark as she spoke, her anger quite obvious. She never told me if she got a chance to tell him how she felt. Amir's death sparked me to cling to Jack more than ever, harsh realities always a firm reminder to speak your mind.

With her statement I knew nothing I could say would stop her from going in, which meant Jack and I went too. We stuck together from the beginning, and nothing would change that.

Jack cursed under his breath. He was too good for our fucked-up existence.

"I'll go with her. You can stay here and call me if more bad nasties show up." I smiled sweetly at him. He and I looked at each other for a solid minute, his expression softening as I smiled.

Windsor laughed and started to say something, I raised my gun again.

"Or I just kill you now and we all walk away." I stared him down as if he were my greatest enemy. "Not a word unless its life or death critical. Clear?"

"Enough of this shit." Destiny turned and went for the door. Jack and I followed close at her heels, the others just behind us.

The interior of the building smelled like dust. Well, the building itself did. The overwhelming rotten flesh stink came from those *things* inside; blocking whatever chance there would be of identifying if something else lurked around.

The unfinished building still mimicked the abandoned nightclub plans, with multiple levels and lots of dark corners. So many things sat half started, bits and pieces clearly stolen and random graffiti covered most of the once cleanly painted walls. Hopefully any homeless and other vagrants that took up residence here vacated the premises.

We walked the expansive main floor as a group, checking every corner and dark area, anywhere something could hide. Destiny took the front, Jack and I flanked her, and the others took the rear. We cleared buildings like a military team, even though we lost key members. Windsor's statement being *one drops, another slides into their place*. He'd have to get a batch of new recruits soon, they probably started gathering.

My anxiety began to prickle up the back of my neck as we ascended the stairs. Hiding my straight up fear in these situations felt like second nature so we all continued on without pausing. Jack and I occasionally made eye contact but that was it.

Could he see in my eyes how terrified I was?

I wanted to hold his hand, for us to turn around and run off into the sunset together. I was *so* over this life. We could run out the back door and disappear; Windsor taught us how to hide. If we really wanted to and made the effort even the great Order of Nevar could never find us. But we'd leave our families behind, which we'd do anyways if we ended up dead.

We cleared the first room quickly and approached the door to another. Assuming it would be a similar layout to downstairs, we knew the space and its size. I could sense movement beyond the closed door, shuffling and thumping that came with walking around.

Destiny stood closer to the door and listened. She gestured four to us; there could be more but that's what she heard. She grabbed a tiny vial from her pocket and clutched it tightly. The stun bombs I made were sometimes helpful but not always. I made sure I held one in my free hand; my gun tightly clutched in the other.

Destiny glanced at all of us again, raising her arm up to signify time to get ready. When she looked satisfied, she dropped her hand, kicking the door as hard as she could.

The door crunched and flung open, bits of splintered wood burst into the air. Destiny walked in, gun drawn, and tossed the stun bomb into the middle of the room.

I heard the shatter and explosion, and then Jack and I followed her. No time to think, barely even enough time to breathe. As soon as I passed the doorway I threw my stun bomb, going after the first body I saw.

Clicking and shifting echoed through the room as the enemies moved around us. Not pausing to look for weapons, I advanced. Too much indecision could cost me. I grabbed my branding coin from my pocket and dove on the closest body, which hissed and burned when the coin touched their forehead.

Hideous red eyes turned to me, saliva dripping from its mouth as it snarled with disgusting teeth. I'd been lucky enough to catch it sitting, using my height and the angle of my arms to keep it down for now. The foam coming from its mouth looked pinkish red, like it fed recently.

It twitched, a quick movement as it went to try something, but I moved faster and shot it three times.

Two to the chest, one to the head, just like Windsor taught us, and it exploded into dust.

Moving on to the next one I destroyed two more before looking at my surroundings. We were ok, with enemies exploding left and right. I smiled for a moment.

A thunderous crack and slam made me jump as a door hidden behind a curtain burst open. An enormous beast of a man, who I knew I'd seen before, trampled into the room like a rhino and headed straight for Destiny. His face looked covered in pock marks and boils, as if the skin dripped like wax. His biceps rippled so big his shirt might rip at any moment.

I screamed Jack's name and ran for her, ignoring the gunshots and roars around me. Big man picked up Destiny by her long glossy black hair and grabbed her throat. Her pretty green eyes bulged as she gasped for breath.

Pulling another stun bomb from my pocket I launched it directly at his fat face with no effect. Without thinking my gun went up and I fired at him, I put four into him including two head shots. Before the second head shot made contact, he clenched his fist around her throat, her eyes swelling more as he pulled. With a sickening rip and blood shooting everywhere like a confetti explosion, he tore out my best friend's throat and tossed her body on the floor like a used tissue.

Running to her, I hit the ground and pulled her into

my lap. She stared up at me as she gasped for air; blood poured out from her throat and bubbled from her lips. I took her hand and squeezed it as hard as I could over her gaping wound. Trying to steady myself, I did my best not to hyperventilate.

"I'm so sorry. I love you." I sobbed. She mouthed a word at me that I couldn't understand. I leaned down and managed to hear her say, "Survive" before she stopped moving completely.

"Kennedy! Kennedy! We have to go!" Jack shook my arm violently as it hung lifeless at my side.

"I can't leave her!" I wailed.

"If we don't leave *right now,* we're going to die too. You can't kill Windsor if you're dead!" He grabbed my arm and pulled me up. "Frost! We have to go!"

Setting her down softly, I kissed her forehead and stood. We went for the door big man came from, jumping over his body. A quick look around as we slammed the door behind us let me know that Jack and I were the only ones left standing. Several big men came in from other doors, whoever watched the exits sucked balls.

But that was it, wasn't it? No one watched the exits.

We grabbed everything we could to barricade the door, pulling furniture and boxes until we felt confident it would hold long enough for us to make a plan.

The butt of my gun scratched my forehead as I raised my hands; it felt cold and centered me. When I looked around the room I started to hyperventilate more, and things became fuzzy, and I felt a little lightheaded.

With random furniture piled around, we must have been in some kind of storage room. The only other exit being a small window about ten feet up.

"He lied to us *again.*" I repeated, not loud enough that I thought Jack could hear me.

"Technically I don't think he did." Jack began grabbing pieces of furniture and piling them along the wall under the window. "But we'll debate that later. First, we have to get out of here. That means I need you with me."

He grabbed my free hand with his, our guns still gripped in our other hands.

"Kennedy. I need you to focus. We have to climb up and crawl through that window." He gestured upwards. "You can freak out later."

"How can we just leave her like that?" I blubbered.

"Just like we had to leave all the others. Because you'll die! We'll die! We HAVE to GO!" He screamed in my face. "Can you kick out that window?"

I looked up, and at the pile of furniture he stacked for us to climb. "Yeah."

He popped out the clip on his gun and checked inside, cursing under his breath.

"What?" I asked. A loud thump shook the door and we jumped.

"Nothing. Go!" He dragged me over and pushed me up the stack of furniture. With my gun tightly gripped in my left hand I climbed up, and I got close enough that I could grab the windowsill.

Luckily the window folded open, and we could easily

pull up and slide through it. I looked down at Jack, who guarded the door with his gun in his hands.

"We don't have to kick it. It folds open." I pulled myself up like doing a pull up. "C'mon. It will hold. Let's go."

Dangling my legs out the window, I slid out until my body hung against the outside wall and my hands tightly gripped the windowsill. I tried to look below me, and it appeared to be a straight drop, so I let go. Broken ankles and getting eaten flashed before my eyes as I zoomed down.

I got lucky and landed on my feet. Backing up, I stood in the shadows and waited.

Time seemed like it stopped, and I went into full on panic mode. We discussed repeatedly what to do in this situation, but I could not remember any of it. My mind went completely blank, barely forming a coherent thought.

I would wait a few more minutes then go back in and get him. I may not get to choose about her, but I *would not* go without him.

My mind raced with all the possible outcomes when I saw his feet and legs come out the window and his body rapidly fall to the ground. His face looked battered, and his nose started to swell. Blood droplets spattered across his skin; his big green eyes looked wild.

"I'm ok." He pleaded as I pulled him to his feet. "That door didn't hold as long as we thought."

"We can discuss tactics later. Can you walk?" I asked.

Jack limped forward a few paces. "I'm good. Let's go."

We started towards the open end of the alley where we encountered a row of dark figures.

"Windsor may not have lied but he sure as shit didn't do anything to help us." I snapped.

Without another thought I held up my gun and started firing.

Not wanting to waste bullets, I stopped and pulled two large hunting knives out of their holsters at my waist. Jack kept his gun raised as I held my blades in fighting stance.

Two of the figures came at us so quickly we barely had time to react. I stabbed one, the blade sinking in what felt like Jell-O. Reaching out to grab the one closer to Jack I slashed into it before it touched him.

He shot it twice in the upper region; we still couldn't see any faces. I heard one of them say something like 'order scum' before they all dissipated as if they were made of smoke.

Grabbing Jack's arm, I dragged him out into the open. We were back by the front entrance; I saw no sign of Windsor anywhere.

"Looks like he cleared out. I got a pretty good idea where to look." I turned and gasped when I saw Jack. His free hand held tight across a huge gash in his stomach. It looked as if some of his insides were hanging out. Why didn't I notice before?

Pulling him back inside the alley, I sat him down with his back against the wall. Trying to assess the damage in the dark proved tough, but his fingers clearly were tangled in something. I put my hand on top of his and pushed against his wound. It squirted more blood, coating my hand and starting to run up my sleeve.

"I'll call an ambulance." I went to pull my phone out of my pocket.

"We both have loaded handguns." He watched me as I fumbled around like an idiot. "And there is a bunch of dead bodies inside."

"I don't care."

He laughed. "Yes, you do. I'm not worth it."

"Yes, you are."

He touched his fingers to my cheek, smearing it with blood. I leaned forward so our foreheads met. His skin felt warm.

"That's the nicest thing you've ever said to me Frost."

"I should have said it sooner. I should have screamed it from the rooftops."

"It's not because I'm dying?"

I smiled; my vision blurry with tears. "Of course not you idiot."

Jack coughed; his face grimaced in pain. His beautiful perfect face. I should have told him all the time how I really felt. My foolish pride stopped me from being honest. I would regret that for the rest of my days. Maybe this would be my last day.

"I can't do this without you." Hot tears started to flow down my face. He pushed his gun into my hands, placing them both above my heart.

"Take my gun and use it to kill Windsor. Promise me you'll go and do it now."

My heart started pounding, anxiety grabbed hold of me with a vice grip. My mouth felt dry, my tongue like sandpaper. Tears poured down my face.

Jack coughed again. "Go, Kennedy."

"I won't leave you alone!" I took the gun and put it in my waistband, then sat beside him with his hand clutched firmly in mine. I thought briefly about his mom, who loved him so much. She should've been here. If this moment was destined to happen it should have been somewhere nice, not a dirty dark alley.

He smiled, and then coughed again. "You have to survive. You're the one, Kennedy Frost."

"How do I do this alone? I'm not strong enough."

"Yes, you are." He sputtered. "You are the strongest of all of us. You have to do this for all of us."

I leaned over and kissed him softly on the mouth. "I love you so much. I'm so sorry I couldn't save you."

When I pulled away his head fell limply to the side, his eyes blank and empty. My heart broke at the thought that maybe he hadn't heard me.

With Jack gone, only I remained.

My insides screamed. My logical brain kept saying to call an ambulance. Maybe there was a chance. Maybe there was still time, on the off chance I could be the hero and save him.

It took me a while of just sitting for everything to sink in. I took a deep cleansing breath and my training kicked in. Emptying his pockets, I shifted him so only his beat-up Chuck Taylor's could be seen when you looked down the alley. Moving his head around, I tried to make it so his eyes looked at me. Even if Jack no longer looked back, maybe his eyes could one last time. But it didn't work.

His eyes would never look at me again.

My heart began to hurt in a way I never felt before. Like it was eating itself and leaving a gaping hole in my body.

Reaching into my inside pocket, I used the bandana I kept for this purpose to wipe him down, removing my fingerprints. I wrapped it around his ring, slipping it off his finger and putting them both back in my inside jacket pocket.

I stood, putting my gun away and making sure my jacket covered his when I tucked it in my waist band. The cold metal touching my skin felt good. It centered me and gave me the confidence I needed to walk away. Windsor discussed this with us at great length; even he expressed this would be the hardest thing we would ever do, even harder than killing.

Keeping to the shadows, I moved slowly and calmly into the night. After about ten minutes I called the police.

Two guns.
Nine bullets.
Two knives.
One stun bomb.
Three vials of kerosene and a lighter.
It would have to do.

The official headquarters of The Order of Nevar sat under the library of the downtown campus of the University of Toronto. There were many other locations around the city, including my high school, but this acted as ground zero. My group and I discussed the age of the building, and whether they built it with the intention to put The Order in the basement or it came later.

Most of the entrances were unguarded. Unless you knew what you were looking for, they were just ordinary doors, and they didn't think they needed to guard them. Good for me.

Keeping both my guns hidden I went in, starting down the winding staircase. I saw no one; the thump of my sneakers provided a rhythmic noise for me to concentrate on over the pounding in my ears.

Pushing through the big wood doors, I walked into the empty main meeting room.

All the recruits were dead except me, only the higher ups would be lurking around. If Windsor ran back when shit went south, they would all know by now. Hopefully they were having a moment of silence somewhere.

Carved with ornate filigree and mystical symbols into dark cherry wood, the inner office doors looked like something out of a movie. They made my skin crawl, like I stood before the Temple of Doom.

Standing outside them always meant something was coming. News, trouble, orders.

This time, that something was me.

Channeling the energy of my best friend, I kicked the door open. The big wood panels banged on the walls with a thud, but it didn't splinter or even crack. I wondered how many times this great door got kicked in such a fashion. Windsor and two of his high priestesses jumped from where they leaned over the desk, their bare asses exposed to Windsor. The large dark wood surface dominated much of the room; it looked like the set for an old school vampire flick.

Jack loved every inch of the room. I pushed the ache for him aside.

Windsor's eyes grew wide as dinner plates. "Frost! I'm…"

"Surprised to see me?" I grinned from ear to ear. The dried blood smear on my cheek cracked as I moved my mouth.

"What happened?"

"What do you think happened? Your intel was bullshit. *Again.* I think you did it on purpose."

He chuckled. "It's not *my* fault. We staked out…"

"Yeah, you mentioned that. And you didn't stick around long enough to guard the doors." I stood about a foot away from the desk, hands on my hips. "I think you played us. You got in Destiny's head and amped *her* up, knowing Jack and I would follow. They tore her throat out first." I pulled out my gun and cocked it. "Jack and I almost got away until we got jumped in the alley next to the building, after having crawled out a tiny window. An action *you* could've prevented if *you* bothered to stick around and guard the perimeter. He literally held his own guts in."

Windsor sighed loudly, like I somehow inconvenienced

him. "I don't know what you want me to say Kennedy."

"Let's start with *I'm sorry*."

One of the priestesses went to move towards me and I pulled Jack's gun from my waist band. "You don't have to die too."

"Listen to me, Frost..." Windsor began, slowly beginning to stand.

"I'm done listening to you. Consider this my official retirement." I barely got the words out when out of the corner of eye I saw that same priestess move and I shot her in the head without blinking.

Everyone else froze when her body thumped to the floor.

"Now that I have your attention." I put a bullet in Windsor's right shoulder, and he plopped back down in his chair. Two shots meant security would be coming. "I want to hear you say it."

"Say what?" His voice sounded panicked. "What do you want?"

"What do I *want*? *I want my friends back.* I want you to say you're sorry they're *all dead!*"

I shot him in the other shoulder. "Two to the chest, just like you taught me."

He looked up at me from his seat behind the desk and I saw nothing in his eyes. I knew in that moment no matter what anyone did or said he would never feel anything for the countless numbers of teenagers who died under his tutelage.

Something inside me always knew, and he never did anything to make me think otherwise.

"You know you'll never walk out of here." He tried to keep his breathing calm.

I laughed loudly. "Is that a joke? I am the strongest you ever had, by your own admission. And I have two guns. If it's my time to die, so be it, but I don't think it is."

He began to breathe heavily, snarling out. "I did my job, Frost. What do you expect?"

"They all died, and you don't even care. How many were there before us? Hundreds? How many have to die before you give a shit?" Before he could reply I put a bullet between his eyes.

The other priestess attempted to dart past me, looking for any chance to run. I grabbed her before she got to the door.

Holding tightly to her throat, I squeezed until her eyes watered than shoved my gun in her face. The hot barrel made a strange sound on her skin. A scar would be a constant reminder.

"You tell them." I growled in a low voice. "Tell them Kennedy Frost is *done*. Do you understand? And if they come looking for me, they will regret it. Are we clear?"

She nodded quickly and I released her. Watching as she ran out, I stood alone again, but I knew the others were with me. Wiggling my fingers by my side, I imagine Jack coming up beside me and taking my hand as he did so many times before. I needed to really drive my point home; Jack would have called it something clever like dotting my i's.

I searched the room for ingredients, and within ten minutes the room went ablaze, and I'd found Windsor's keys and phone.

Fire had a way of cleansing all your sins. I could wipe my slate clean.

With the rising sun, it finished. Every location of the Order of Nevar that I could drive to burned. At each location I found someone, one person left to say my name to the others and tell my story.

The name Kennedy Frost would now live in infamy among their ranks.

The strongest.

The survivor.

The final girl.

ACKNOWLEDGMENTS.

This book came together differently than the others. Mostly because the world around me has changed, I thought it was time for a change.

I know you're probably wondering, dear reader, if this is the end for our intrepid little prophecy girl, and I can assure you it's not. It's only the end of this part of the story, with much more to come. Thank you for taking part up to this point and I hope you continue on this new path. 2001 is just a small taste of what's to come from the world of Camille Bishop.

I want to take a little time to thank RM Gilmore, whose sound advice and wisdom have kept me going through so many levels of crazy I don't know where to begin. Thank you, Tara Dawn, for always being a shining light in the darkness.

Thank you to my father, Lawrence Maurice, for his

editorial assistance and words of encouragement. I am overwhelmed with joy to have you along on this journey.

Thank you, as always to my husband Michael, for not thinking that I'm crazy and keeping me sane in this insanity.

And thank you again, dear reader, for coming back and hanging out with me. Show your love for Camille and any book by leaving a review anywhere you make your purchase

ABOUT RAVIN TIJA MAURICE

Ravin Tija Maurice lives in Mississauga, Ontario, Canada with her husband and daughter.

Her books span several time periods and feature a diverse cast of characters, all with a paranormal twist. She loves to binge watch television shows, has a large collection of stuffed animals, and is a history geek. A lifelong writer, she is constantly trying to find ways to grow and learn new skills.